Also by Alison Tyler

———

Best Bondage Erotica

Best Bondage Erotica 2

Exposed

The Happy Birthday Book of Erotica

Heat Wave: Sizzling Sex Stories

Luscious: Stories of Anal Eroticism

The Merry XXXmas Book of Erotica

Red Hot Erotica

Slave to Love

Three-Way

Caught Looking (with Rachel Kramer Bussel)

A Is for Amour

B Is for Bondage

C Is for Coeds

D Is for Dress-Up

E Is for Exotic

F Is for Fetish

G Is for Games

H IS FOR HARDCORE

EROTIC STORIES
EDITED BY ALISON TYLER

CLEIS
PRESS

Published in the United States by Cleis Press Inc.,
P.O. Box 14697, San Francisco, California 94114.

Printed in the United States.
Cover design: Scott Idleman
Text design: Karen Quigg
Cleis Press logo art: Juana Alicia
First Edition.
10 9 8 7 6 5 4 3 2 1

.

Acknowledgments

Hundreds of Hurrahs to:

Felice Newman

Frédérique Delacoste

Violet Blue

Thomas S. Roche

and SAM, always.

Pleasure of love lasts but a moment.

Pain of love lasts a lifetime.

—JEAN-PIERRE CLARIS DE FLORIAN

contents

INTRODUCTION: HAVE YOU FOUND IT?

HAVE YOU FOUND what you're looking for?

Was it what you expected? What you thought you deserved?

Personally, I'm still on a quest, searching. But at least I know what I *don't* want. I don't want nice and clean. I don't want good and kind. I want hot and fast. Dark and dirty. Basically, I want hardcore.

But what does that word mean? According to the authors in this book, hardcore is something different for every person.

From Radclyffe:

"I've done sweet. Now I want something else."

"Like what?"

I twisted both rings until my nipples wouldn't stretch any more without tearing. The pleasure and the pain fused into a fierce ache in my clit and my knees nearly buckled. He watched my face, and I knew he knew I was struggling not to moan. "I guess that will be up to her."

And Teresa Noelle Roberts:

His hands were calloused and a little dirty—slurry from sharpening blades, perhaps—but when he caressed my face and down my throat, tracing the line of the jugular vein, I moaned deep in my throat, imagining the same delicate touch from a knife, just skimming my skin, hinting at a million possible deaths without doing any harm. I arched against him.

And Jean Roberta:

Carla sighed. "Poor, brainless man, you must help me to untie her and place her in a more suitable position. I can use one of those belts to better effect." Amy's mouth went dry.

But the common thread from one story to the next is the search. The search for something dark. The search for something dreamy. The search for something more.

The search for something hardcore.

XXX,

Alison

MATHILDE MADDEN

ME, WHEN I'M WITH YOU

HARD COCK, HARD MAN.

You're standing over me as I lie on the bed. It would almost make me feel weak and small if I didn't have such an incredible hold over you. If I hadn't taken you to the edge five times already today. If you didn't need to come so much right now that it's pulsing off you.

You're naked. You're so pretty when you're naked that all I really need to do is look at you. Strip you and have you stand there while I masturbate to the sight of you. Use you as porn.

But today, God, not today. Not with the way your breath is stalling, the way your shoulders are moving; the way your aching, wanting cock is hitching forward, fucking the air in front of you. Your hands are braced behind your neck. You know better than to move them.

"Lick your lips," I say. So cheap, but it makes me hot to see your tongue because it reminds me of all the times I've used your tongue as a sex toy.

Your tongue moves over your top lip. You keep eye contact with me, like you're trying to seduce me. Maybe you don't realize you don't need to. Don't realize how helpless the sight of you like this makes me. Maybe you don't feel how much power you have over me. Maybe all you can feel is how much you need to come. How much you need to convince me to let you come. Really, I don't need convincing of anything.

I lean over and pick up the cuffs that are lying on the floor and hold them out to you. You move your hands from behind your neck and take them.

"Put them on."

You snap each bracelet around a wrist and take a careful moment to fumble and flip the safety catches that stop them getting tighter. I love you in handcuffs. Your thick wrists look weirdly oversized in them. You make them look tiny and tinny. Like jewelry. Sexy boy. Sexy decorated boy. It's not even Christmas.

Clamps would be nice, too, I think. More sparkle. Clamps are pretty. Your pain is pretty. More than pretty. But I'm too much of a greedy needy wanting demanding bitch right now to stop and look for them.

So instead I say, "Touch it. Touch yourself."

You do it. You put your cuffed hands on your cock. And you moan. You actually moan. God, you are such a tease.

You know just how to make me want you. And I start to think about letting you come even though that isn't my plan. I think about how your face looks when you release. My pussy starts to pulse harder. And it was already on fire before.

I make myself tell you to stop, and you give this delicious twisted little noise and put your cuffed hands back behind your neck.

I don't know how I am supposed to maintain a demeanor of icy control in this situation. I'm so completely the opposite of icy. I'm so damn hot and so damn wet and all I want to do is tell you to come over here and fuck me as hard as you can.

Some people do this kind of thing all day long. Every day. Tease men. Dominate men. Some people do this for a living. How do they not lose their minds? Maybe because they don't have you. That's what I keep telling myself. They're not teasing *you*.

Your hips are still jerking a little. I think about getting off the bed and kneeling in front of you and taking your cock in my mouth. I love your cock. I love sucking your cock. It took me a while to find a suitably dom way of sucking your cock, but eventually I discovered that if your hands were tied behind your back and your ankles were forced apart with a spreader bar and your nipples were clamped and I had a vibrator tight against your arsehole, that worked for me. Kneeling in front of you when you're trussed like that. Like some kind of ripe, throbbing bondage god. Long licks; teasing, swirling my tongue around the head. Making you see stars. So yeah, I can suck your cock and still be topping you. Which is nice. Because sucking your cock and owning you are my two favorite hobbies.

But I'm not going to suck you now. Delicious as your cock looks, you're just too ripe for teasing.

You're looking right at me. Naked. So hard. Big muscular legs spread, hands behind your neck. Oh, God, you're so fucking hot. I want to come. I could come just looking at you. I already said that, didn't I? Well, you haven't exactly got any less hot since then, you know.

"I'm thinking about your chastity belt," I say. You manage to avoid making a noise. You sort of swallow. Actually, it's like a gulp. It's delicious. You really don't know I'm lying. That there is no way I could strap you away at this point. I'm lost. You've got me. You've totally got me. But you don't know it and I lie to you some more. "I'm thinking about strapping you away instead of letting you come. You could beg me not to do that, if you want."

You say something like, "Please don't," but it's really quiet and simply won't do.

"I didn't hear you," I say. "I need to hear you."

Your tongue flips over your lips. Fuck. Your tongue. You make me think of that tongue on my clit. You make me want you even more. I can't take much more of this. "Please," you say, more loudly than before. "Please don't do that. Don't. I can't. Please, baby, I want to come."

I dig my fingernails into my palm.

"I don't know," I say. "It really is so hot when I strap your cock away. Hide the key somewhere and wait—what?—a week, until you simply can't do anything except beg me on your knees to let you free. Until you reach the point where you'll scream with frustration if I so much as blow on it."

"Baby," you say gently, "baby, I'm already there."

Sometimes, I'm so in the moment, so in control or at least in some semblance of control and you say something like that, something soft, and it's all I can do not to come crashing down. When you say that, with your voice all gentle and pretty, I want to hug you. I could drop

— 4 —

right out of role any second. Crash. Bang. I can feel it. This is getting serious. Who's driving this thing? I need to find an endgame. And fast.

I sit up and scrabble around among the debris on the floor for the key to your handcuffs. It takes me a couple of moments but I find it. I beckon you over, and you step forward, bringing your wrists from behind your neck so I can reach them.

I unfasten the cuffs and say, "Turn round. Put your hands behind your back."

You turn around slowly with one slight moment for a pause and a quizzical expression. Your cock bobs as you move. It's so hard and angry looking. It looks painful. It's got to be really sensitive. Sensitive like I can't even imagine. I reach up and recuff your big wrists behind your back.

"Turn back around."

You turn to face me, cock still vicious angry.

I say, "Get on your knees now."

You go down, big man. One knee then the other. When you kneel, it dismantles me. Every time. It's like I have to wait and let myself crumble then put myself back together and carry on.

Now I'm sitting on the edge of the bed with you kneeling in front of me and my pussy is just burning. What I'd really like to do is grab you by the hair and pull you tight between my legs. I'd like to do this so sudden and fast that you don't really have time to catch your breath. So fast it hurts you enough that you make a confused little yelp and you aren't sure what is happening for a long moment before you realize your world is made of me.

I don't do it.

I deserve a fucking medal.

You're kneeling on the floor surrounded by all the Tracey Emin–style crap that accumulates by the bed when you come to stay. There's chocolate and the nipple clamps that would have been good to put on you a bit earlier—but it is so too late now. There's a gay porno magazine that you brought me and all your clothes. You've been naked for two whole days. Sometimes when I look at you naked I want to burn your clothes. You were made to be kept naked.

It's been two days. Two days naked and hard and you still haven't come.

All the crap on the floor is mostly on the rug. I slip off the bed and pull the rug out of the way, leaving a stretch of bare floorboards next to you.

I sit back down. "You still want to come?"

"Baby?"

"Do you?"

"Yeah. Yes."

"You reckon you can make yourself come like this?"

You're kneeling naked on the floor with your hands cuffed behind your back. But I'm sure you are pretty aware of these facts. You look at me, but there's no need really, because you know I mean it. You know what I'm saying to you. What I'm telling you to do:

"You're going to have to fuck the floor if you want to make yourself come." I wait. I let you hesitate a little longer, and then I say, "Or we lock it up."

Your chastity belt is clear plastic. We bought it online ages ago and we hardly ever use it. It's fiddly and annoying and mostly we just never bother. But it works well as a threat. It was worth every penny for that alone.

You lower yourself onto the floor. I don't know quite how you manage it with your wrists cuffed. Maybe just sheer force of will. I look at your arse. Your hands curled in the small of your back. Your hips move. Start to pump. It's just bare floorboards under you. You must be so sensitive. It must hurt, but the way you're moaning suddenly, it must be working, too. You're fucking the floor and moaning like you're inside a lover.

Like you're inside me.

Fast and frantic suddenly, you move like you've lost it. Maybe you think I might tell you to stop at any moment.

Maybe I will.

No. No, I won't.

I want to see you come like this. You must know that. If you thought about it you'd work that out.

Your head goes back and you pump your hips hard and roar and scream. God, that was quick. I'm disappointed. But then I think about what you've just done and I almost come myself. You just fucked the floor to get yourself off.

I can't believe you just did that. I've never wanted you—or anyone—so much in my whole fucking life. I want to roll you over. I want to straddle your chest and rub my crotch against your hard nice abs until I come myself. I want to twist my fingers in your hair and pull your head up and make you look me in the eye. I want you to know that I just watched you do that. And that I got off hard on it. I want to get down on the floor and lick your come up myself and push it down your throat with my tongue. I want to hurt you and kiss you, write on you. I want to lock you in a cage and starve you.

Sometimes I don't know what I am or what you've made of me. I want to watch you dying. I want to stare at your mouth forever.

TO PROTECT and SERVE

ARD AS STEEL, EIGHT INCHES. That's what I was packing. Other men quite often looked at me with intimidation in their eyes, and that was just fine. That was what I wanted. It was what Lynn needed.

Lynn McCain, sexy siren of a brunette, with classic lips and classic hips that harkened back to Jayne Mansfield. Back when women were women and men were lucky to be allowed to bask in the ripe presence. Lynn is a powerhouse vixen who emanates sex everywhere she goes.

I am the man who is always there, always following her, always standing in her shadow. I am the one man on earth she cannot live without. Literally.

I am Lynn McCain's bodyguard.

Since Lynn first lit up the silver screen, I have followed her across the globe. I have watched photo shoots in Singapore and runway shows in Milan. I have dined with the royal family of Morocco and fought through a throng of photographers in New York City. I have been on private jets, even more private yachts, and once in the bedroom of an international star whose name shall never be mentioned—but trust me, the rumors are true.

I have been there to watch it all.

Because I am a bodyguard, I am often a shadow. I am often ignored by everyone nearby and that is a good thing. Blending into the background is crucial. No one should notice I am there until they make a move on Lynn. Then they are very well aware of my presence, usually when I have my knee pressed into their abdomen, my hand in a death grip on their throat, and my pistol against the underside of their rib cage. I can take a clear shot without getting so much as one drop of blood on Lynn's thousand-dollar stiletto pumps.

I had to do it once. You might remember the headlines: The actress who was almost killed by a deranged fan. The fan was shot and killed on the spot by a quick-acting bodyguard. The story didn't focus much on the bodyguard because stories about shadows don't usually sell tabloids. That bodyguard was yours truly.

I've shed blood for Lynn. Someone else's, and my own: I took a bullet to the arm that day. It sliced right under my tricep. There is a scar and an ache when it rains, just to remind me that I'm tied to Lynn for good. I will always be the man who took the bullet for her.

Sometimes bodyguards fall in love with their clients. Depending on the level of maturity in that love, it can mean the death knell to the relationship in more ways than one. A bodyguard can never get too comfortable. When protecting someone like Lynn, I have to be constantly on my toes. The only time I can unholster the gun and the mentality that goes with it is when I am locked away in that big Georgian mansion behind those big iron gates, when the other security guards take over and I am free to go to my little collection of rooms in the east wing of the enormous house. That is my day off. That is the only time I can be a man and not a machine.

Those are the times Lynn spends the night in my bed.

No one knows this, of course. No one but me and Lynn. When we are in public or even among her bevy of servants, she treats me like the shadow I have to be. I would tolerate nothing more or less than that, for my sake and her safety. But when those gates are locked and those big double doors are closed, Lynn comes to my bed and gives me what all those who gaze at her with lust in their eyes can only dream of having.

It's been going on for a year now. For the last six months, there hasn't been anyone but me. I know that for certain because I know everything she does, down to the time she takes her shower and how many hours she spends on that expensive cell phone of hers. There was a time when she was fucking me for the sheer fun of it and then fucking other men as well. Once there was even another woman.

Lynn always made me watch. Knowing someone is jealous over her gets her hot as hell. It always got her off to ask me if I liked watching some young stud go at her. The truth was I hated it. I hated it because it turned me on, too, and as soon as that young stud was out of earshot I would be fucking her myself.

Once I took her in the back of the limousine right after she left another man's apartment, breaking my own rules of discretion and constant vigilance. Her skirt up just enough, my slacks unzipped, my gun rocking gently in the holster with every thrust, I took her right there on those fine leather seats, and I covered her mouth with my palm to keep her moans from letting the driver in on our little secret.

Since that night, there has only been me.

I know it is probably a mistake. I know it is probably putting us both in jeopardy. A bodyguard has to find the balance between too much and too little. He has to walk that thin line that keeps him close but not too close. I've crossed that line, I know. But I really had no choice, you see. Lynn made sure of that.

She had become comfortable enough not to bother disappearing into another room to make herself presentable in the mornings. I learned that the barely awake, slightly grumpy, and tangled-hair Lynn was much sexier than the polished, brightly smiling woman on the screen. My discretion and sense of decency had made her more and more open, and gradually I began to see her wrapped in nightgowns, pajamas, even once in a towel. She caught me looking and blushed. The next time she didn't blush and just smiled. I should have known then what was coming.

Lynn began to taunt me. At first I thought I was imagining things. But one day she stepped out of the bathroom wearing nothing but drops of water. The invitation was evident, and if I didn't get it from the mere look on her face, the sultry "Come to bed" was as clear as it ever gets.

I was going to decline. Really. I was. But then she kissed me and that was it. The woman can kiss like nobody else on the face of this earth. Soft lips, just enough tongue, and those breathy moans that say she's enjoying this just as much as you are. It's the kind of kiss that makes strong men feel weak all over.

One kiss, and five minutes later she was sliding down on my cock. I was in awe until she came and then I was enamored for life. When she came, her whole body flushed pink, like someone turned on a light inside her. I make it a point of watching her do that as often as possible. It's really something to see.

To top it all off, Lynn is into kink. Last night she was really into kink. It's a good thing that today is my day off because I need the time to recuperate and think things over.

Just as I know many personal things about Lynn, she knows a few very personal things about me. She came upon a stash of my porn magazines not long ago. What she was doing in my private rooms, I didn't even think to ask. She raised an eyebrow while she dangled one of the magazines in front of my face.

"You're into this?" she purred.

I blushed furiously when I realized what she was holding. It was a magazine filled with men who were taking it up the ass. From other men, from women with strap-ons, from groups of women with all sizes of dildos.

All I could do was nod. What was the point in lying?

I should have known then what tricks Lynn had up her sleeve.

It was late at night when she came to me. I was naked in bed, almost asleep and thinking about her. I heard her moving in the darkness, and I instantly tracked where she was, the way a bodyguard always knows where everyone in the room is standing. Then I heard a noise I hadn't heard before. A tinkling sound, almost like handcuffs.

My guard went up immediately. The one thing I do not let Lynn do is use handcuffs on me. Ever. There is still too much of the protector mentality, even during those most intimate times. I have to be able to move quickly and at a moment's notice.

"You're not using those on me," I said into the darkness. Lynn stopped moving. I could almost hear her smiling. Her voice was low and coy.

"Oh, I think I can change your mind."

I shifted in the bed and started to reach in the direction of the voice. She found me first. She slid her hand up my thigh and found my cock. I was already rock hard at the thought of having Lynn in my bed again. She took advantage of it by rubbing me with long, firm strokes. I heard the tinkle of metal again.

"No," I said, and Lynn chuckled. She took my hand and led it down…down, between her legs. I jerked back at the surprise of what I found there. Lynn sighed a happy sigh and turned on the bedside lamp.

Lynn McCain, the sexy siren who has made millions of hearts flutter, was standing in front of me wearing a strap-on cock. The look was completed with a gorgeous leather bustier and leather boots. But it was the cock that held my rapt attention. I watched as she stroked her cock slowly while she looked me in the eye.

"I'm going to fuck you with this," she said.

My own cock immediately went from hard to diamond-cutter stiff. I took a deep breath and my voice didn't even sound like my own when I spoke. "Will you be gentle?"

She considered my request with a gleam in her eye. "I'll use lube," she conceded. "And you will wear this."

She held up a cock ring. It had a larger ring that was supposed to fit around my balls. I shivered in anticipation. "If I can't tie you to the bed," she said, "at least I can tie your cock up."

I lay back and watched as she slid the leather over my cock. It chafed a little but she didn't seem to care. She pulled it tight around my balls and when I grimaced, she just pulled it tighter. It was quickly becoming apparent what I was going to go through. Whether it was the ring or Lynn's roughness, I found myself harder than ever. I longed to stroke my cock and more than that, I wanted to feel what I had dreamed about for as long as I could remember. I wanted to feel that cock slide into my ass. I wanted to come that way.

I watched as Lynn opened the bedside drawer and pulled out the little bottle I kept there. It had only been used for those rare times she let me slide my cock into her tight little ass, or those nights when I had to take care of things myself. She held the bottle up in front of me and smiled a naughty smile. "Get on your knees, bitch."

I hesitated. I wasn't used to giving up control for anyone, even for Lynn. I knew she had a dominant streak in her, but I had never catered to it until now. I was nervous as hell. Lynn stepped forward and grabbed my hair, a quick motion that was completely out of character for her. I stared up at her in surprise.

"Get on your knees or I might change my mind about the lube," she taunted.

I scrambled to obey, then I watched Lynn as she circled the bed, stroking her cock all the while. I heard the little click of the bottle opening. Then I heard the rude noises it made when she squeezed some of the lube out. When she touched my ass, I jumped. She ignored my moan of concern and spread my cheeks so she could spread the lube where she wanted.

I got even more excited when she rubbed my asshole gently with her finger. Then she pushed a little and one finger slid inside. I had played with myself like that before, sometimes using two fingers before I came, but it felt different to have someone else do it. I pushed back against her hand and Lynn purred in approval. "Good boy," she said.

She pumped that finger in and out for a while, talking to me the whole time. "You really want this cock up your ass, don't you? You want to feel it stretch you open and then slide all the way in. But do you want me to go nice and slow, or do you want me to fuck you hard and make you hurt? Which one do you want?"

I groaned as she fucked me harder with her finger. "I want it hard," I whispered.

"I can't hear you," Lynn said menacingly.

"Hard," I responded, and I felt myself blushing again, just like I did when she found my porn magazines.

"Tell me more," she demanded.

"I want it hard…I want you to fuck me deep. I want you to slide it in slow so I can feel the way it burns. Then I want you to just let go and fuck the hell out of my ass."

Lynn got up on the bed behind me. She played with my ass for a while longer. I jerked and moaned and tried to take more of her finger inside by leaning back on her hand. I could hear the sound of the lube as she stroked her cock.

Then Lynn got on her knees and poised herself right behind me, pointing her cock at my rear entrance. "Take a deep breath," she said softly, and I did. I held on to the pillow for dear life. I knew she was going to be careful but I knew it would hurt anyway. The funny thing was, I wanted it to hurt. I felt like it should. Giving up your virginity shouldn't be easy.

Lynn slipped the cock between my cheeks. She ran it up and down across my asshole. The tip of the cock slid against my balls every time she stroked downward. I wanted to come so badly, but the cock ring was tight, almost too tight. I knew I wouldn't be able to come until Lynn let it happen. I felt completely controlled by her. Lynn lifted one leg to make the angle better. Now she was leaning over me, kneeling with one knee on the bed. She had more power that way, too. She could slide into me with one long stroke and put all her weight behind it. I was filled with a kind of delicious terror at the thought that she just might do that.

She just might make it very memorable.

Lynn pressed the tip of the cock to my tight asshole. She began to push. I felt my sphincter open up a little and it felt good at first, but then it began to burn. I clenched the pillow and buried my face in it so that I wouldn't tell her to stop. Lynn stroked my back gently. "Push back against me," she said. "It makes it easier."

I was sure she knew what she was talking about. I had fucked her ass enough. I bore down as if I were trying to push her out. To my surprise, she slid in farther. The burning was more of a sting now, and I knew that was the feeling of her stretching me to take her cock.

"I'm going to take you," she whispered, and then she thrust forward. I felt the head of her cock pop through the rosebud of my ass. I cried out and my cock jerked. I needed to come so badly but I couldn't, not with that tight ring around my shaft. The burning sensation intensified as Lynn put her weight behind her cock and slid it halfway in. She got down on her knees and braced herself behind me.

"Does my big bad bodyguard like taking it up the ass?" she taunted.

"Yes…don't stop, Lynn. Don't stop!"

Then she started to fuck me. She slid all the way in and then pulled almost all the way out. It stung like fire, but it felt incredibly good. Her thrusts pushed me down on the pillow, and I lay my head against them while she plowed into me from behind. My balls swayed with every plunge. My cock throbbed. I felt her cock rubbing deep inside my ass. One thrust sent jolts of pleasure though my body.

"God, I need to come!" I moaned. Lynn chuckled at me.

"I'm going to ream you out until I come first," she said. "You should see your pretty little ass, all open and begging for this cock. It looks so good disappearing in there. Does it hurt?"

Lynn went at me harder then, and I couldn't have answered her if I wanted to.

After a few minutes she slowed slightly, then reached down and stroked my dick. The need to come was starting to get painful. Lynn leaned over and whispered in my ear that she was going to fuck me as hard as she wanted and she was going to come while she did it. Then she was going to release the cock ring and make me come all over the bed while she plundered my ass.

"But you have to beg me," she said.

So I started to beg. "Please, Lynn. Please fuck me as hard as you want. Come while you do it. Come, baby, please come. I'll do anything you want, just come and then let me come too. Please, please…"

Lynn slid in and out a few times, nice long strokes that got me ready for what was going to happen next. Then she thrust in hard. She grunted with the effort. I cried out loud and clenched the pillow. I was begging her to let me come. I was begging her to fuck me harder. Then Lynn plunged deep and let out that cry I knew so well, that cry that said she was coming, and coming hard.

I wished I could see her face while she did it, but more than that I wanted some relief of my own. I wanted to come while that cock sawed in and out of my ass. Lynn rode out her orgasm, pushing a little with her hips to get that cock as deep into me as it would go. Then she leaned over and caressed my balls.

"You want to come, baby?"

"Yes, please!" I was almost delirious with the need. She rubbed my cock. I felt her fingertips on the snaps of the ring and suddenly I couldn't breathe.

Lynn smacked my ass. I yelped. She pulled halfway out and then thrust in deep. Finally, she pulled on the snaps and that cock ring gave way. The long-denied orgasm seemed to start in the middle of my spine and drive itself out through the tip of my cock. I came so hard, it hurt. My whole body shook. I said things but I'm not sure what they were. I was incoherent, basking in pleasure. I heard Lynn laugh from above and behind me, and she was still plugging away at my ass, somehow making the orgasm last even longer. I shot jet after jet of sticky semen onto the sheets.

Lynn thrust into me one more time, then slowly pulled out. I collapsed onto the bed, smearing my belly with the come I had just left there. I hardly noticed. My ass burned and throbbed with every beat of my heart. I had the very distant thought that if anyone chose to attack Lynn right now, right here in this bedroom, they could just have at it. Some bodyguard I was. I was too drained to move.

Lynn curled up beside me and stroked my back. Her fingertips traced warm trails from my shoulder to my hip and back up again. I closed my eyes.

"You liked that," she said. It was not a question. I grinned against her shoulder.

"I'm glad you found those magazines," I admitted.

She snuggled up closer and pulled a blanket over us. She was almost asleep when she spoke again, and from her voice I could tell she was smiling.

"You're just as good a lover as you are a bodyguard."

I chuckled. "I'm just here to protect and serve."

RADCLYFFE

SWEET NO MORE

AVING SECOND THOUGHTS?"

"No," I told Phil, my best friend from work, for the tenth time.

"Okay, then." He said something I couldn't hear to the bouncer on the door and then motioned me inside. We paid our cover at a window in a closet-sized vestibule, and Phil pushed aside the black vinyl curtain blocking the entrance to the club. "Have fun."

The minute we walked into the Ramrod, Phil and his boyfriend melted into the crowd, and I was on my own. I couldn't complain. They said they'd bring me; they never said they'd babysit. I hadn't really thought places like this existed anymore—a warehouse-sized room illuminated by black lights, with rough brick walls, exposed pipes in the ceiling, pounding bass beat, and wall-to-wall bodies, mostly naked and, at first glance, mostly men. Bare chests, pierced nipples, chaps over naked skin, straining cocks beneath codpieces and jocks. I felt overdressed in my leather vest and pants, even though I had nothing on underneath either one. The place smelled like stale beer, acrid poppers, and the musky odor of sex.

Lots of sex.

It was exactly the kind of place I fantasized about while I jerked off, picturing what I *thought* might happen so many times it was getting tough to come that way anymore. I needed the real thing—or maybe I needed something I hadn't yet imagined. Trying to look like I belonged, I wended my way toward the bar. I shoehorned into a place at the bar and worked not to stare at the guy standing next to me while another guy knelt in the cramped space and sucked on his cock with gusto.

"Beer," I shouted when the bartender glanced in my direction.

The guy next to me grunted, and I automatically looked over just in time to see him yank his cock out of his buddy's mouth and pump it frantically, his face a twisted mask of concentration. Then he smiled at me half-apologetically and came all over the guy's chest.

"Nice shooting," I observed and reached for my beer. I drank half of it off to steady my nerves.

"Thanks," he gasped after he caught his breath and wiped his hand clean in the other guy's hair. "You alone?"

I kept my gaze on his face, but I could hear the guy on the floor whining as he jacked off. From the sounds of things, he was about to unload a gallon so I inched away to keep the stuff off my boots. "Came with friends, but I lost them already."

"I brought a friend, too." He looked me over. "You a novice?"

"No," I lied. "Why?"

"Because she's not."

My clit shot out an inch and turned to marble. "Sounds just right."

He didn't look convinced. "What are you looking for?"

"I'm not here to look." Praying he couldn't see my hands tremble, I unbuttoned my vest and uncovered my tits. They were small and round with neat dark areolas, which made the silver rings through the center of each nipple all the more obvious. I gripped the rings and pulled, tenting my nipples until they turned white. "I've done sweet. Now I want something else."

"Like what?"

I twisted both rings until my nipples wouldn't stretch any more without tearing. The pleasure and the pain fused into a fierce ache in my clit and my knees nearly buckled. He watched my face, and I could tell that he knew I was struggling not to moan. "I guess that will be up to her."

"I'm Jerry." He stuffed his limp cock back into his pants and sidled away from the guy slumped on the floor. I hadn't noticed him shooting, but the puddle between his legs and the come splattered on the bottom of Jerry's pants lit up like neon under the lights. "Follow me."

I didn't bother to close my vest. I was just another body. Besides, my nipples were engorged after the twisting and so sensitive that if they rubbed against the leather vest now, I'd have to go somewhere and jerk off. I wanted to anyway. My clit was pounding as if I'd been working it for an hour.

We went through the bar and down a hallway and into another room. The only music now was the grunts and cries and moans of people fucking and coming. Jerry paused for a second, then said, "Over here."

He led me toward the far side where a leather sling hung from the ceiling by chains. A young blond guy with smooth pale skin reclined in the sling with his head thrown back and his legs bent up while a dark-haired guy whose face I couldn't see stood between his legs, a fist up the blond's ass and the other hand jerking the blond's jutting cock. The guy doing the fucking was slender with finely muscled shoulders and a hairless back that tapered into a narrow waist, and he wore nothing but chaps that left his high, round ass exposed. His sweaty skin glowed beneath the lights as he rotated his forearm in the blond's ass and worked his cock like a piston.

The blond raised his head and stared at the hand jerking his cock, his face dazed and his stomach heaving to the beat of the fist in his guts. "I'm gonna blow," he hissed.

The guy fisting him never stopped pumping the iron-hard dick as come arced into the air, the first shot hitting the blond's chest then dribbling into little puddles on his belly. A third guy leaned over and licked up the blond guy's come, then took two steps back and shot his own load in the blond's face.

"Jesus," I whispered, my clit twitching like crazy. I needed to jerk off now more than ever and wondered if I could just go lean against the wall like a few other guys I could see were doing and get a quick shot off.

"That's his lover," Jerry whispered, pointing to the guy who'd just blasted off in the blond's face.

"Who's their friend?" I asked, tipping my chin toward the dark-haired guy who eased his hand out of the blond's ass, stripped off a glove, and tossed it on the floor.

"That's who I want you to meet."

Before I could reply, the fister turned to face us, and I was looking at a woman so hot I forgot all about my stiff clit and needing to jerk off. Her eyes were dark like her hair and her expression remote, as if she hadn't just fucked some guy for an audience. She had smallish breasts about like mine and stomach muscles that were etched and pumped from the workout she'd just had. Her mons was trimmed, not shaved, and framed by her chaps, which was all she was wearing. From what I could see of her cunt, it was swollen and shining with come. If she hadn't gotten off during the fisting, she must really need it bad now.

"Ask her if I could please suck her off," I said desperately to Jerry, having no idea what the correct protocol was, but I didn't care. "Ask her please. Anything she wants if I can just suck her clit."

I stood still while Jerry made his way to her and said something. Then she stared at me for a long moment before walking over. I didn't say anything as she held open the edges of my vest and stared at my breasts. She flicked one nipple ring with a long finger.

"Are these for show?"

"No," I croaked.

She unzipped my leathers and slid her hand down my pants. I sucked in a breath as she explored my clit with one finger. After a minute of that I started to sway, but I was afraid to touch her to steady myself.

"What do you want?" she asked, dragging her fingertip up one side of my clit and down the other, over the head and back again.

"I want to suck you off."

She pulled her hand out of my pants and I fought not to whimper. "What about that pretty little hard-on you've got in your pants?"

"I'd like to come for you," I whispered. "I'd like to come for you harder than I've ever come for anyone."

"Any way I want it?"

"Yes."

She gripped my wrist and dragged me through the crowd, past the sling where she'd fucked the guy, to the corner where a padded pole a foot thick ran from the floor to the ceiling. She stripped off my vest and dropped it on the floor, slammed my back up against the pole, and jerked my arms around behind it. I felt her buckle leather shackles on my wrists before she came back to face me. She yanked my pants down to my ankles and kicked my feet as far apart as they would go.

"Is there anything you want me to know?" she said, rubbing her palms in rough circles over my breasts, bringing my nipples screaming back to life again.

"I don't fuck men."

"What else?"

"I'm not sucking anybody's cock."

"That's it?"

"That's it."

She grabbed my face and shoved her tongue into my mouth. I couldn't breathe, so I bit her, just hard enough to make her ease back. Then I sucked her tongue until *she* couldn't breathe.

She pulled out and licked my lips like she wanted to eat them off my face, flicking her tongue into my mouth too fast for me to catch it again, although I snapped my teeth and tried. She laughed.

"You think I'd waste these sweet lips on a cock?" She bit my lower lip and twisted my nipple rings. I whimpered. "I'm saving your mouth to come in myself."

Breathing fast, she rubbed her cunt on my leg. She was hot and slippery and her clit was a hard knot in the center. "I'm going to drown you in juice."

She kept at it, rubbing and sliding, until she shivered once, hard, and jerked away without coming. My cunt was spilling and I was drenched to my knees with her come and mine. She forked her fingers, clamped my clit in the vee, and squeezed.

"Fuck," I whispered, sagging against the pole.

"You've got a nice fat one, don't you?" she murmured, jacking me slowly. Too slowly to make me come but enough to make me need to so fucking bad tears leaked out of my eyes. She pinched the head with her nails and I did cry. "Poor baby. Let me make that better."

"Please," I begged, all pride washed away in the sea of blood pooled in my cunt. I wondered if I was supposed to resist, but I didn't care now. I just wanted to come.

She pulled something off the waistband of her chaps at the same time as she spread my cunt open with one hand. I couldn't see much, but when I looked down, my clit was standing up between her fingers. Even in the dim light I could tell it was wet and the dark color it got when I was about to come. If she jacked me now, I'd shoot.

She did, and my legs started shaking and my clit got extra hurting-hard, the way it did when I was ten seconds from coming.

"I'm almost there," I said because I thought I should tell her, but she must have known because she stopped cold. "I'm about to come...please."

"Breathe, baby," she whispered, and before I knew what she was doing, she replaced her fingers on my clit with a two-inch spring-loaded clamp. It closed onto the shaft of my clit with a snap and the rows of blunt teeth dug in and banished the blossoming orgasm into oblivion.

I screamed.

"Shh, shh, shh," she crooned, her mouth on my neck oddly gentle as she licked the sweat and tears that ran down from my face. She rubbed my lower belly, pressing into me in deep circles that somehow made the profound ache inside almost bearable. "Does it hurt, baby?"

"Yes," I whimpered. My cunt throbbed like someone had kicked me, and needles of pain speared through my clit.

"You've got a beautiful clit," she whispered, jiggling the clamp with one finger. "Look how big you are now."

I bent my head and tried to see, but the tears clouded my vision. My clit pulsed between the jaws to the beat of my heart, and I felt something else, something even more powerful than the pain. "I need to come."

She flipped the clamp back and forth. The pressure surged in my clit and my cunt opened and closed like a fist.

"Oh, fuck, that's so fucking good."

She gripped the clamp and twisted.

"I want to come so bad."

"And I want you harder. Harder than you've ever been for anybody." She pulled my nipple ring and jacked my clit with the clamp. The teeth dug into the hood and pulled it back and forth over the head with every tug—pleasure, pain, pleasure, pain, pleasure, pain. "*Now* you might be hard enough to shoot a nice load for me."

"I don't think I can," I moaned. The clit torture wasn't hitting me right to get me off. "I really need to come."

"Watch me do you, baby."

I tightened my stomach and bowed forward, shaking sweat from my face so it wouldn't run into my eyes. My clit was stretched out, impossibly swollen, the head bulging beyond the clamp. Seeing her fingers, slick with my come, tugging the clamp was too much. "Oh, God, you don't know how bad I need to come. I think my clit's gonna burst."

"Now it might," she said, and pulled off the clamp.

Blood rushed in, my clit doubled in size. The nerves in the head short-circuited from the sudden stimulation. Pain and pleasure blasted up my spine in equal measure. I thrashed and tried to get loose. I had to hold it, rub it, do something, anything, to stop the agony.

"What's the matter," she whispered, fingering my nipple rings rapidly again.

"I gotta come," I howled. There were more people around us now, most just staring, a couple jerking off. I didn't care about them. I didn't care about anything except coming.

"Let me help you." She fingered the head and, oh, God, it hurt. It was so good and it hurt and I wanted to come so much and it hurt and I couldn't and I was fucking dying.

"Oh, Jesus, don't touch it!" I moaned. "It's too hard now. It hurts. Oh, Jesus. Fuck." I was blubbering, tossing my head around.

She seized my face again and forced me to look into her eyes. "Shut up and breathe." She kissed me, so gently I felt like she was rocking me in her arms. "I'm gonna make you come, baby, so sweet."

She kept kissing me, her tongue delving deeper and deeper until I was sucking it again. Then I felt her fingers glide over my clit and my body jerked. She rubbed it and it felt so good and I moaned. She backed out of my mouth and straddled my leg, her wet cunt hot enough to burn my skin. She whimpered and I realized how long she'd been holding back.

Some guy close to us groaned, and I could hear the frenzied slap of his hand on his cock, and she growled, "Shoot on the floor, cocksucker, not on her," and he did.

"Get ready, baby." Then she lowered her head and took my nipple in her mouth, chewing on my nipple and tonguing the ring while she switched her grip on my clit and started to jack me. With so much stimulation happening everywhere at once—her cunt, her fingers, her mouth—the pain in my tortured clit didn't prevent the orgasm from building this time. My clit couldn't get any harder, but it started to throb inside, and the pressure spread into my belly, and I knew nothing was going to stop me.

"I'm gonna come," I cried, and my cunt started to spasm.

She shoved her fingers into me and raised her head to stare at my face. "Give it to me." Her palm thudded against my unyielding clit as she fucked me, and I unloaded into her hand and over her arm, crying and yelling *Oh fucking God it's so good…*

She didn't quit until there wasn't a drop left in me and I was twisting to get away from her fingers, my clit so fucked out I wasn't sure I'd ever need to come again. She reached behind me and released my hands and I fell to my knees, trying to drag air into my lungs. She didn't care if I could breathe or not. She grabbed my head and tilted my face up and jammed her clit into my mouth.

"Now suck me off," she ordered through gritted teeth, her clit like rock and already jumping. She bucked her hips and pumped her clit in and out of the circle of my lips, jerking herself off in my mouth.

She was starting to come, so I sucked her just hard enough to keep her clit in my mouth. I wanted it to last for her.

"Here it comes, baby," she gasped, her fingers trembling in my hair. "Get ready to swallow. Sweet baby, you're making me come."

I clutched her ass and yanked her hard against my face, sucking her clit in to the root and clamping my teeth around it. She cried out and ejaculated on my face and I felt her legs go. I wrapped my arms tightly around her thighs to hold her up because I knew she would hate to go down in front of everybody. When she stopped coming I licked up the juice that clung to her cunt and tongued her clit until she murmured a protest and pulled away.

Somehow I got my legs under me and heaved myself to my feet, hauling my pants up with me. My clit was still so tender I couldn't zip them. The dark-haired girl backed me into the pole again and leaned her arms on either side of my head so she could lick her come off my face. Her whole body trembled, and I risked putting my arms around her.

"That was sweet, baby," she whispered so no one else could hear.

I kissed her and she let me, and as I played my tongue inside her hot mouth, I realized that I had been wrong about what I had been looking for. What she had given me was sweeter than sweet.

JOHN A. BURKS, JR.

CONTROL

IS LIFE WAS ABOUT CONTROL, power…domination. It didn't matter if it was at home, with the perfect wife and the perfect kids who worshiped him, or at work, dictating to the board of directors of a Fortune 500 company. It didn't matter where Benjamin Friar was, control was the only issue that mattered. It was what separated man from the animals. Power was absolute.

Not that having his secretary bent over the mahogany desk, panties around her ankles, his cock in her ass, was much different than the animals.

"You like that, you dirty little bitch?" he asked, already knowing the answer. There was a reason he'd hired the voluptuous blonde and it wasn't her typing skills.

"Yes, Mr. Friar," she replied, gasping for breath, "more please."

Helen didn't really like anal sex. He knew that, but making her say it…that was control, just as having her face shoved against his day planner, mascara and sweat leaving a black stain across his Thursday ten o'clock, was control.

Benjamin thrust harder, savoring the sound of the flesh of his thighs against the fatty part of her ass. "I know you do. All my little whores like it in the ass."

The secretary shifted, grabbing at his cock with her cheeks. "Yes, Mr. Friar, fuck me harder."

He savored the discomfort on her face and relished the thought of her walking funny the rest of the day. He pumped harder, quicker, nearing climax, as the phone on his desk rang.

"Fuck," he spat in disgust, pulling out and reaching for the phone. The moment had been lost, his control broken by the chirping of plastic and electronics.

"Mr. Friar?"

"Yeah, maybe later, sweets," he told her, smacking her on the ass. "You sure? I still have a few minutes before my break is over."

He waved her away, picking up the phone. "Later."

"Have you really lived?" the voice on the other end of the phone, dark and rich and most definitely female, asked him.

"I'm sorry?"

"It was a simple question, Mr. Friar."

He started to hang up, but the woman's voice was intriguing. "I'd like to think I have."

"You tasted flesh of every continent on this small world, Mr. Friar, sampled every delight you've ever desired. You're CEO of one of the largest telecom companies in the world, having made your first million at the ripe old age of twenty-one." The woman paused, and Benjamin imagined her taking a deep drag on a cigarette and blowing smoke into a darkened room. "You've done and seen more than most men twice you age, but have you really lived?"

He squirmed uncomfortably in his leather chair. The person on the other end of the line knew more about him than he'd like. "Who is this?"

"You still haven't answered the question, Mr. Friar. Are you fulfilled? Can you die today and be a happy man?"

"Yes," Benjamin replied without hesitation. He was at the top of the world. What else could there be? He was master of all he saw.

"That's too bad. I thank you for your time."

"Wait," he demanded, hesitating. "What's this about?"

"This is about fantasy, Mr. Friar, and fulfillment. Possibly fulfillment of fantasies you don't yet know you have."

"That's silly. How could you fulfill a fantasy I don't have?"

Again the woman paused and his imagination ran wild. "Is it not equally silly to write off something you have no clue of?"

It was Benjamin's turn to pause. "Okay, say I bite. What does this cost me?"

"Always to the point, right, Mr. Friar?"

"Yes, to the point. How much?"

"That's entirely up to you. Payment is not due until the end of the service. You pay what you feel it was worth."

"You're kidding, right? What if I'm not happy? Hell, I could just say I wasn't happy."

"There's only one way to find out, Mr. Friar."

Her voice captivated him and it didn't take long for him to agree. She gave him a time and a location, said good-bye wistfully, and his mind raced, yet there was concern. He wasn't in control here. Far from it.

But something about that tantalized him, and he could think of nothing else as he slipped away from the office early.

The blue-collar bar stank of cheap liquor and cigarette smoke. It wasn't the sort of place he'd normally be caught in, but this was different. He understood this could be a strange sort of setup. His wife knew of his habits, of course. How could she not know of the trips to the Costa Rican whorehouses, the calls in the middle of the night, the lipstick on the underwear? Benjamin supposed she might finally be fed up, anxious to exert her own control over the situation, but having the imagination to do something this elaborate, just to prove his philandering ways, was beyond her.

And besides, who did she know with a voice like that?

"Mr. Friar?"

The man behind him was a walking wall covered in the graffiti of one too many trips to jail. His face was impassive and hard.

"That's me."

"Come with me, sir."

The big man turned toward the back door, and Benjamin hesitated. What if this was some bizarre kidnapping scheme? He shook his head, dismissing the thought. It could be a thousand things other than what the crimson-voiced woman on the phone had said it was. He had no control.

And that scared the living shit out of him.

The bar's back door opened into a small alleyway, moonlight making dancing shadows of the piles of garbage and empty beer cases.

"Say, if this is a fucking blow job behind a bar...sorry, I'm not interested."

Benjamin didn't see the fist as it slammed into his face, driving him backward. He tried to struggle, but the vice grips locked around his arms and a black bag was forced over his head.

"Relax, Mr. Friar. If you struggle I'll have to make it rough for you. Not that I necessarily mind making it rough, but Ms. Michelle won't have anything to do with it. Not her precious customers, no."

Michelle. A name with a voice. A voice with a promise.

But fear overwhelmed the desire to see the face connected with the voice, "Please..."

The big man chuckled as he tied Benjamin's hands behind his back. "Please what? Don't hurt you?"

A powerful hand gripped his wrist, pain and numbness flaring through his hand. "Just realize *I'm* in control here, Mr. Friar. If you misbehave and displease Ms. Michelle, I'll have your testicles."

The big man thumped him in the crotch, just hard enough to make him jerk, to emphasize his point.

The passage of time was meaningless as his wrists throbbed from their bindings and the van hummed through the city streets. Benjamin had no idea where he was, nor did he have any idea how many sets of hands, once they'd finally reached their location, lifted him from the van and laid him on his back. The hands were gentle but firm, untying him and then stretching out his arms, affixing them to planks of wood running crosswise from his feet to the opposite arm in an *X* shape. His legs were outstretched similarly, and as his pants were removed, he felt every inch of his nakedness.

"Welcome, Mr. Friar." He heard that voice, the voice of a sex goddess, as the hood was pulled off.

She stood before him, nearly six feet tall, with long vibrant red hair that seemed to have a life of its own, and legs to dream about at night. She was dressed, if the word *dressed* could be applied to her skimpy outfit, in the barest of red sashes, not bothering to cover her firm full breasts and large pink nipples.

"I…" Benjamin stuttered, unable to bring his eyes from the object of the afternoon's fantasy.

"You do not speak, Mr. Friar. Only I speak here. Do you understand?"

"Yes," he gulped and then cried out in pain as the cat-o'-nine-tails lashed out, striking him broadly across the chest.

"There is punishment for displeasing me. First, it's the simple whip. A few lashes here and there." She struck out at his thigh, leaving raised red welts across the pasty flesh. "Continue to displease me and it's Frank."

Michelle gestured to the large man whose fist Benjamin's face had already met.

"Just to put it out of your mind, yes, Frank likes to hurt people. Isn't that right, Frank?"

"Yes, Ms. Michelle."

"I believe he enjoys it even more than I do."

Benjamin's heart pounded like an old Chevy with timing issues as the wooden frame he was strapped to was raised by half a dozen young women who wore nothing more than silk masks.

"There are also rewards," Michelle told him as she stepped forward, her right hand grazing up from his navel to his left nipple. "Rewards with the pain." She pulled on the nipple and he gulped.

"That's how you work, isn't it, Mr. Friar? Pain and reward? Control and domination? A man like you doesn't get where he is without knowing those things."

She released the nipple and slapped him hard across the face. "Life is about power, yes? When you get to your position in life, there is little else."

Benjamin wanted to see her hurting, his cock in her ass and her begging for him to stop.

"Anger is good. It gets the blood pumping," she said as the whip lashed out again, striking him across his softening belly. "But why are you angry, Mr. Friar?"

The whip lashed out again and he clenched his teeth.

"I'll tell you why you're angry. You're angry because I'm in control."

"No. I'm angry because I fell for this silliness. Angry with myself."

The whip came down again, harder, scorching his chest. He arched his back and groaned. Michelle then dropped the whip and grabbed his testicles with her left hand, the other hand expertly tying a red satin sash around them.

"I told you, Mr. Friar, you do not speak here. This isn't your board-room, nor is it your comfy little house with your perfect wife and perfect kids. This isn't even your secretary taking it in the ass because she wants a raise."

"How do you know these things?" he asked, ignoring Michelle's threats.

She sighed, reaching down to the floor. He couldn't see what she was doing between his legs, but he heard the strike of the lighter and smelt the candle. "A question here, a question there. Surely you know it's a good idea to research potential clients. You just don't seem to know when it's a good idea to shut up."

Benjamin couldn't remember ever screaming as hard as he did when the wax dripped onto his bound testicles. He screamed until he couldn't scream any more, straining against his bonds, pulling at the silk that tied him to wood.

"You are nothing here, Mr. Friar. Nothing to me. In reality, you are nothing at all to anyone. You don't really have any power, Mr. Friar. None. I could kill you here, right now, and what would happen? Do you think they'd ever even find the body after Frank had finished with it?"

Two of the silk-masked young girls stepped forward, simple wooden clothespins in their hands. As Michelle withdrew the candle, they affixed a pin to each nipple.

"Do you know what true power is?"

She nodded and the girls placed two more. Not nearly as serious as the pain from the wax, but enough to make Benjamin flinch. "Pain, Mr. Friar. Pain is the only power worth exploiting."

Again a nod and again another pair of clothespins. He finally cried out on the sixth set, the burning and stretching of the skin around his nipples too much to take. Michelle only laughed.

"Please…" he whimpered.

"Please more?" Michelle said, igniting a cigarette with the same lighter with which she'd lit the candle. "Please more, *ma'am.*"

Another of the six girls kneeled behind him, and he could feel the spreading of his asscheeks and the wet sound of lubricant on flesh. He gasped as the plug, thin pointed and wide based, was inserted.

Michelle leaned over him and stroked his face. "You see, there can be pleasure, Mr. Friar. Pleasure in pain. You like a cock in your ass, don't you?"

"No," Benjamin said, squirming against the uncomfortable pressure in his ass, the pins on his nipples, "I don't. Please…let me go."

Michelle knelt and removed the plug, but replaced it with her finger. She probed gently, pushing toward his prostate. "I'm sure, Mr. Friar, if you'd had a cock up there, at some point, you might understand. You like the other way around, no?"

Amid all the pain, the humiliation, and the fear, something stirred, as if the gentle pushing of her finger had reached beyond just his ass. His cock began to rise slowly, and the smile that spread across Michelle's face was pleasing. Her tongue darted out and lapped at the edge of his growing erection.

"That's right, Mr. Friar. There is pleasure in pain." A gentle nod of her head and one of the girls picked up the candle, letting the wax drip down over his cock. He pulled back at first but then steadied his mind, letting the pain become pleasure.

"There is ecstasy in losing control, life in being on the other side," Michelle told him, removing her finger and replacing the butt plug. She took a length of soft nylon rope and began feeding the end to one of the naked girls who looped it around his legs, running it all the way up both. He could see his erection pulsating now, the restricted testicles making it seem much, much larger. Once the rope was around his waist, Frank reached forward and pulled, the loops tightening around him until his flesh threatened to burst underneath.

"There are sensations you've never known, Mr. Friar, simply because for your entire life you've refused to let go. That's all you have to do, Benjamin. Let go."

The veins in his legs bulged all the way to his cock. Michelle grasped it firmly in her hand, and he could feel every inch of her flesh on his, unlike anything he'd ever felt before. She stroked his cock softly, up and down, slowly, and Benjamin gasped, no longer from pain but from sheer ecstasy. It only took a few more silent seconds of stroking from Michelle's hand before the climax rushed forward from his testicles, stopped at the binding of silk. With a simple flick of her wrist she undid the small tie, and Benjamin's head throbbed with stars. It was the most powerful climax he'd ever had.

The room was silent for a few moments as his body went limp, completely drained.

His arms were freed, the nylon rope and clothespins removed. One of the girls washed the lubricant from between his asscheeks after she removed the butt plug. The lashes across his chest were tended to, and the girls helped him slip into a soft white robe. Later, as he was soaking in a steaming hot bath, Michelle joined him, her legs intertwining around his.

"I hope the experience was all that I made it out to be, Mr. Friar."

He nodded in agreement. It was, and he'd already envisioned an amount of money for payment greater than a lot of people made in a year. "Just one question, though."

Her eyebrows raised as she leaned forward, smiling. "Yes?"

"Next time do I have to be kidnapped? Or can I just show up here?"

JEAN ROBERTA

IN THE HOLD

H ONEY, DO YOU THINK she'll find a buyer for the house?" Amy
asked. She lay with her head on Michael's chest, her long brown
hair in a silky tangle under his nose. They were entwined on his
king-sized bed, which dominated the one small bedroom in his basement apartment. The place was less a love nest than a temporary
refuge along the highway of Michael's life.

Amy was trying to make the best of things. She didn't want to think
about Carla, Michael's brisk, sharp-featured wife, but her image invaded
Amy's mind whenever she tried to imagine her future with Michael.

"If she beats the bushes," he sighed. Amy had met Carla before
she and Michael had given in to temptation. Carla tended to be very
direct about what she wanted. And apparently that was what Michael
didn't want. Not anymore. Amy could imagine Carla beating bushes
to drive a lurking house-hunter into the open and then cornering

him into making an acceptable offer. It was a strangely exciting image.

"Are you sure you don't want to just cut the knot and leave town, alone and free?" She knew how quickly men escape when they feel trapped or hunted. Amy didn't want to rely on false hope.

Michael sat up and savored the sight of his girlfriend's high, pointed breasts, crowned with large pink nipples. Her hair flowed romantically over them, and she looked completely different from a snappy, short-haired wife focused on the spoils of divorce.

The man slipped a wiry arm under Amy's slim waist and pulled her to him. "I'd like to sail the high seas," he growled thrillingly in her ear, "beyond the reach of Her Majesty's laws. I'd be a salty dog with a captive princess on my ship."

Amy squirmed and squealed. "Am I the captive princess?"

"Aye, wench, that you are," he assured her. Michael affected a piratical squint, as though gazing into the future across a boundless glassy ocean. Amy loved this side of him.

Before she guessed what he was planning, he pulled one of her arms to the cold brass headboard and wrapped a belt around a corner post, buckling it around her wrist. She laughed and rolled to her side, reaching up to free herself.

He lowered his mouth to one nipple and sucked it in past his grazing teeth. He flicked it with his tongue, and Amy felt the echoes in her clit. Her hips rocked subtly, as if by instinct, and she lowered her knees.

Michael pulled away, deliberately tugging the nipple in his mouth until it was stretched to an almost unbelievable size. He left it exposed to the air as he seized one of Amy's shins. That was when she noticed that lengths of chain and Velcro cuffs were attached to each of the brass posts at the end of the bed. Michael had carefully prepared for this scene.

"Oh, Captain," she begged dramatically, "what are you going to do to me?"

"Make you a woman, my dear," he growled, showing his teeth. He held one of her ankles and fastened a cuff around it. "'Tis what you need. You will not be satisfied until I do."

"You brute!" she wailed, trying to free her trapped foot. Flashing her a wicked grin, Michael reached for her other leg. As she tried to shake him off, she gave him a clear view of the moist pink lips framed by the curly brown hair between her thighs.

"What a beautiful clam," he told her, stretching out his free arm to slide two fingers into her opening. "With a pearl just waiting to be found."

Amy felt lusciously violated, as though she were really a sheltered virgin whose life could be changed completely through this deflowering. "Oh!" she squealed, not caring who heard her. "Sir! I'll be ruined!"

"Not so," chuckled her ravisher, stroking the very wet folds of her cunt as he steadily sank in deeper and deeper. He added a third finger. "You'll be a pirate's woman. Mine to plunder at will." Just when Amy feared that she couldn't hang on to what little resistance she had left, he pinched and squeezed her clit with his free hand, rubbing it with no regard for its sensitive nature.

"I won't stop, my dear," growled Michael, "until you surrender."

Amy thrashed in her bonds as though she wanted to escape, but Michael hung on for dear life, and her squirming only increased the stimulation of his hard, determined fingers. A merciless orgasm grabbed her in its teeth, forcing a series of moans out of her mouth. The sound seemed to echo off the ceiling.

"Aha," he muttered, almost to himself. For a disconcerting moment, he sounded like everyday Michael until he slipped back into the role of Pirate Captain.

Since becoming lovers, Amy and Michael had never discussed role-playing. Even though Amy, as editor of the college newspaper, had once interviewed Michael, the theater prof, about a student production of Shakespeare's *The Tempest*. He had been the director.

Now Amy was fully inhabiting her own role. She used her one free hand to grab him by the hair so that she could glare into his eyes. "Brute," she reproached him. "Criminal. You have stolen my virtue and now you have to marry me." As soon as the words were out of her mouth, she wished she could take them back.

He seized her wrist with swashbuckling speed. "And so I shall, tempting morsel," he gloated. "You need a husband to master you." To demonstrate his point, he pulled her free hand up to the bed frame, then awkwardly rummaged in the bedclothes to find another belt to restrain her with. He checked her other wrist and noticed that it was red from the rub of leather.

Michael had no qualms about leaving marks on a willing victim, but unforeseen redness on his captive's skin suggested a lack of preparedness on his part. He wanted to seem wicked to the core, not sloppy.

As Amy watched curiously, Michael slid out of bed, opened his underwear drawer, pulled out two pairs of jockey shorts, climbed back onto the bed, and carefully wrapped each of them around each of

Amy's wrists under the improvised leather cuffs. He was so intent on solving the problem that he didn't think about how he looked.

Amy snickered. After all, she thought, as a princess she would have been raised in a castle full of servants who responded to her slightest whim. Watching her slim, naked Michael hopping about to secure her bonds made her feel waited-on.

"Aha," he muttered again, appraising his work. Those two exhaled breaths held a world of meaning.

"You can't keep me here," she told him. It was really a disguised question.

Michael grabbed Amy by the hair so that he could grin in her face. "Wench," he sneered, "you need a better understanding of your position. You are secured in the hold of my ship, and no one knows where you are. Even if I returned you to your parents, do you think they would want a dishonored daughter?" Amy actually felt tears prickling her eyes. "Don't cry," he told her more gently. "I don't care what the rest of the world thinks. I want a red-blooded woman, not a simpering girl. And you showed me how much you love being ravished."

"If you value such compliance," she taunted, "you should let me go and treat me with the respect due to my rank. You should call me 'Your Highness.' "

"Saucy minx," he sneered, "you need to learn several more lessons. And you know how satisfying that will be. For both of us. Do you know how mutineers are punished on my ship?"

"By being tied up?" Her voice dripped sarcasm.

"Flogged," he growled, showing her his teeth. "Until they beg for my mercy. 'Tis a fine sight, my lass, and it does them good."

Michael climbed out of bed once again, searched the top of the bureau for something, and returned with two rubber bands. Before Amy could guess what he planned to do, he was winding one around one of her nipples. The pressure was just enough to focus her attention and keep the nipple in a red, swollen condition. Wrapping up the other nipple went faster.

Amy couldn't help admiring Michael's ingenuity, but she made a vague mental note to talk to him later about sex toys.

She also couldn't help imagining how she would look, tied hand and foot without a stitch of clothing and with rubber bands around her nipples, to an audience of sweaty, unwashed sailors who had not seen a woman in months. Which of them wouldn't prefer to watch her being beaten and used without mercy? And which would hope to rescue her from their captain?

Michael seemed to read her mind. "None here will save you, my lass. Scream all you like, for you'll only be letting my crew know that there's entertainment below decks." He cupped one of her breasts and jiggled it for his amusement. Then he raised one hand and slapped her on the hip, just hard enough to sting.

The sound was startling, and so were the echoes of the slap in Amy's flesh. It was one of the sexiest things Michael had ever done to her, and she groaned.

He slapped her again, directly between her spread legs. He did it awkwardly, but the feeling rippled through her cunt and into her belly. He slapped her there a few more times to improve his aim, each time growing more confident. He could see how she was responding, and her squirming, exciting discomfort made him feel as if he could burst.

She had never seen his cock so hard.

Amy's wet, curly bush seemed to be a magnet for Michael's eyes. "You still have another maidenhead, my dear," he told her. "Shall I tell you where?"

Amy blushed. She wouldn't look Michael in the eyes, so he moved up to kiss her possessively, holding her head so that she couldn't look away. He slid his tongue into her mouth, but she knew he didn't want to take her cherry that way—at least not yet.

"I haven't finished searching your fair body for valuables. And I must explore every inch." He slid down to reach between her legs.

And then Amy got another surprise. Like a magician, Michael produced a butt plug and lube out of nowhere, and he lifted her hips and eased it into her virgin anus. The pressure of the plug in her behind and the bands on her nipples seemed to set up a current that ran through her whole body.

"Michael!"

For a moment, Amy felt as if she might faint. Carla's fluty voice was coming through the thin wood of the apartment door.

"Damn!" he muttered.

"Michael!" whispered Amy. "Don't ignore her, or she'll find a way to get in! You know her. Say something to make her go away."

"Honey," he said, sounding like everyday Michael again. "Stay right there. I'll be right back." He smirked, then, because she couldn't have gone anywhere if she'd wanted to.

Amy watched as he grabbed a bathrobe, not wanting to go out of his way to hide anything from Carla. All the same, he didn't want to be more exposed to her than necessary.

She heard the door open a crack. "What do you want?" Michael demanded. He certainly didn't sound welcoming.

"Michael, I need to know where you put the keys to the safe-deposit box. I can't believe you thought you could just keep things hidden from me. You know I'm not greedy, but what's fair is fair, and—what's going on in there?"

"None of your business."

"Damn it, Michael, if I have to show up with my lawyer every time we meet, I'll do it. You can screw around as much as you like once we're divorced, but until then, your business is my business. Don't make this harder than it has to be."

Amy's position made it easy for her to concentrate on what she was hearing. Filled and restrained as she was, she felt luxuriously helpless, not responsible for her own feelings. At the same time, she felt as if she had no place further to fall.

"Michael!" she called. "Let her in! She knows I'm here anyway!"

Amy heard Carla laughing. "She's right," she said. "It's not hard to figure out. I didn't think you were taking a shower in the middle of the day."

Bondage made Amy so attuned to Michael's moods that she could feel his resentment at being outmaneuvered. So it didn't surprise her when he led Carla right into the bedroom to see Amy lying naked on the bed that he and Carla had shared.

For a long, tense moment, no one spoke. Then Carla's face blossomed into a huge grin as she looked down at Amy, who knew her own look must be as pleading and pitiful as Carla could possibly have wanted. "So that's how you two children play together when you have nothing better to do." A guffaw burst out of her, followed by a series of them. "Wow," she laughed. "Wow. You two. The chutzpah just blows me away. Not the kinkiness. I have a few kinks myself, you know, Michael. But the gall of doing it in our bed."

"It wasn't Amy's idea," blurted Michael. He sounded like a chivalrous schoolboy caught smoking with his girlfriend on school property and trying to protect her from a principal's wrath.

"But she invited me in!" chortled Carla. "Michael, I knew she was your girlfriend. I'm not stupid." She paused. "I knew for a long time that you wanted a submissive little pet, but I really couldn't fit into that cage. We could have worked out an arrangement without going through the legal melodrama, but never mind. I've found some new friends, too, so it might all work out fine. Especially if I get my fair share of things."

Carla walked to the edge of the bed and ran a firm, manicured hand slowly from Amy's collarbone, between her breasts and down her tummy to her bush. Amy's cunt squeezed on its own, and the plug in her butt asserted itself. "Amy," Carla pointed out, "you invited me in." She smiled in a way that suggested a wealth of delightful torment.

As Amy watched in amazement, Carla slid two fingers into Amy's open cunt. She made it clear that she considered herself an invited guest, not an intruder. "Nothing in her," she said to Michael. "I thought you would have left her plugged."

Amy's blush told Carla what she wanted to know. "Aha," she muttered. "This is like a treasure hunt." She quickly found the base of the plug, and pulled it out, to Amy's relief and disappointment. Amy didn't really want to be left empty.

"What exactly did I interrupt?" Carla demanded. The question was aimed at Michael and Amy both.

He recovered quickly, and Amy remembered that he was an experienced actor. "Your Majesty," he purred, bowing and slipping off his bathrobe at the same time. "I am captain of the *Jolly Roger,* privateer on the high seas with your knowledge and permission. I have captured a princess from an enemy vessel. The wench enjoyed being ravished, so she needs further discipline."

Michael's bathrobe lay in a pile on the floor. Carla looked down, smiled, and deliberately stepped on it. She clearly hoped to leave a neat shoeprint on the thin blue terrycloth. "Sir Francis," said Carla in a voice of oiled silk, "wouldn't you like to hold her for ransom? Her father might pay a pretty penny to get her back, and he can afford to fill our royal coffers."

Amy had never seen this side of Carla before.

"Your Majesty thinks of everything," he acknowledged, "especially when money is involved. But she is a ruined maiden, so I fear that she will not bring us a profit."

"You want to keep her," smiled Carla, shrugging off her tailored gray jacket. Amy wondered what she was planning to do once her arms were free. "As your own slave."

"As my woman," Michael corrected her.

"Same smell, different word. How do you want her disciplined?"

Michael shifted from one foot to the other, as though he wished he could keep his private fantasies in a safe-deposit box in a corner of his mind where Carla could never find it. "Aarr," he said halfheartedly. "We're on a sailing-ship, eh? Rebels get flogged."

"For the crew to watch!" she finished. "But you tied her in the wrong position for that if you want to give her ass a good basting.

Captain, you do nothing to secure my confidence in your abilities."

Carla swiftly removed her cream-colored blouse, her tweedy linen pants, and her matching ivory bra and panties. Amy knew that Carla worked out regularly, and she seemed eager to show off her trim, fit body. Her arm muscles were alarmingly impressive. The triangle of hair at her crotch was as dark as the hair on her head. Her breasts were small, high, and round, with paler nipples than Amy's. But then Amy's nipples were being subjected to unusual treatment.

Carla sighed. "Poor, brainless man, you must help me to untie her and place her in a more suitable position. I can use one of those belts to better effect." Amy's mouth went dry.

Working together, Michael and Carla lifted Amy's feet out of the ankle-cuffs and released her wrists from the bed frame. Amy rubbed her arms as the blood flowed back into them. "Please, sir and ma'am," she begged.

"What is it, girl?" Carla couldn't help grinning.

"Would one of you release my nipples as well?"

Michael and Carla both tried not to snicker. "I hope you show suitable gratitude," Carla said briskly, unwinding one rubber band and then the other. Amy's nipples throbbed.

"Now, *Captain*," Carla commanded, "I want you to hold her steady while she takes her flogging. Wench," she explained, "you must lean forward, holding onto the foot of the bed like this." Carla demonstrated. She moved away, and Amy stepped into place, shivering.

Michael sat on the bed, holding Amy's hands on the brass bed frame. His erection was painfully obvious, but his expression was comforting.

"The best bondage is invisible," mused Carla. "It consists of willpower alone." Amy couldn't see what Michael's wife was doing behind her. "Carla—Your Majesty," she burst out, "you're not really going to beat me with a belt, are you?"

Carla stroked Amy's lower back and slid a leisurely hand around each buttcheek as though soothing a skittish animal. "You invited me into this game. Don't you both want to know the worst I'm going to do? Aren't you curious? I don't want to hurt you—much."

Carla stroked Amy's hair and back so hypnotically that Amy relaxed a little despite her fear. "Listen to me, girl," Carla warned. "I could do a lot of harm to you or I could show mercy. Michael, what were you planning to hit her with? Just your hand?"

He didn't answer.

"You see, honey, you were going to get the belt even if I hadn't shown up so opportunely. This will be a learning experience for you."

A belt swished through the air and landed with a slap on Amy's ass. A moment later, she felt the burn. "Oh!" she yelped.

"Arr, girl, you're a treat for the crew to watch," Michael told her, pressing courage into her hands.

"You're such a thin-skinned little princess," sighed Carla. "Okay, three more and that's it." The next lick of the belt felt milder to Amy, but she couldn't be sure if Carla was easing up or if she was getting used to the burn. The next slap was definitely harder, and the last felt like being stung by a nest of hornets.

Amy gasped, tears spilling down her face. "I'm done, Captain, you can let go," Carla told her. She grabbed Amy by the shoulders, turned her around, and held her tightly. "Good girl," Carla crooned into Amy's hair. "I don't mind if you want to be Michael's handmaiden for the rest of your life, but I needed that. You, too. Don't you feel better now?"

Amy realized that she did.

Michael was there to pull Amy into a tight hug when Carla gave her to him. By then he had a raging hard-on to cover quickly with an extra skin of latex and slide into the willing mouth of a captive princess who needed to learn how to give proper blow jobs as one of her duties. Carla watched with pleasure, and Amy knew that she would soon be instructed in other forms of oral service.

Amy was still kneeling carefully on the carpet at Michael's feet when Carla walked behind her to admire her own work. "Your bottom is delightfully red, wench," she said, "as it should be. But I really must teach you and the captain a few things about using the right equipment. I won't call him a cheapskate while you're lost in surrender, but he can afford the investment. So can I. And you're worth it."

Later, as the three new playmates rolled together on the king-sized bed, they really felt like fellow travelers on a vast, scary, and magnificent ocean, far from the laws of the land.

Carla was satisfied with the booty she had been given.

Amy felt deliciously used, owned, and enjoyed. She felt like the juicy filling in a sandwich. And she looked forward to learning her place in the hold of the *Jolly Roger,* a most seaworthy relationship.

Michael felt like a salty dog. He was not afraid to put on the bonds of wedlock for a second time, knowing that not all bondage is the same.

SOPHIE MOUETTE

DON'T MOVE

H ELL YES," I SAID, when Emily pointed to a picture of a bound woman and asked if I thought she looked hot.

"Could we try that sometime?" she wondered next, and I had to try so hard not to sound like an overexcited teenage boy that all I managed to get out was, "Really?" Emily's words, Emily's unexpected request to try something new and a bit kinkier than our usual fare hit me like some kind of drug rush. Bottle this feeling and I'd be rich.

"Really. At least…I think so," she said. "Don't you think she looks hot like that?" She waved the picture at me again.

Wrist-to-thigh cuffs held the pretty model's hands in place by her sides, and her legs were cuffed at the ankles, spread wide, and then obviously tethered to something not visible in the picture. It was in our favorite sex toy catalogue, so her sex was discreetly covered by PVC panties, but under the shiny black covering, she had to be open, ready to be eaten or fucked.

Eager for it, according to my imagination.

It was a great image, made even lovelier by substituting my girlfriend for the model. Emily's long red hair would be tousled and tangled from writhing within her bonds—playfully pretend-struggling that was really squirming in pleasure—her skin sleek with sweat, her pussy slick and dripping, ready for me.

The idea shot straight from my brain to my cock, which twitched toward erection at record speed.

"I'd love to," I told her, pulling her (catalogue and all) onto my lap so I could press my hardening dick against her and let her feel how much I liked it. "You'd look beautiful like that. And I'd love having you at my mercy like that. Helpless, unable to resist." I caressed her breasts through her tank top until her nipples popped out, dark and stiff behind the thin, light-blue fabric. Returning the favor, she made small circles with her shorts-clad butt, teasing at my erection.

"I couldn't," she purred. "Resist, that is. I'd be all open and wet and you could do anything you wanted to me." Then she giggled and, turning, kissed the end of my nose. "Not like I resist you all that much, anyway, but I really like the idea of giving you control once in a while. Been working up the nerve to talk about it for a while, and the picture gave me a prop to use. But…"

Her voice trailed off, and she stopped moving. I could feel her body tense, and not in a good way.

"But?" I put my arm around her.

"But at the same time it's scary," she admitted. "Not the giving-up-control part. I trust you, and I think that could be a lot of fun. But I've never actually been tied up, and...what if I freak?"

"Is this something like your thing with planes?"

She muttered an almost inaudible "Yeah." It wasn't exactly fear of flying that kept Emily on the ground; it was the feeling she was trapped on the plane. If someone had issued her a parachute and told her she could jump out any time, though, I think she'd have been fine.

"So you wanted to feel controlled—but not necessarily confined?"

She nodded eagerly.

Worked for me. Sexy as the bands of leather looked against the model's skin, and fun as it might be to tie Emily up in some theoretical world where she wasn't claustrophobic, what I really found arousing was the idea of a woman voluntarily open and helpless to my whim, with or without bondage. And that gave me an idea.

But then Emily turned in my lap until she was straddling me, rocked forward, pulled her shirt off...and somehow we didn't get around to trying my idea that afternoon, but we did test the limits of that particular chair in some interesting ways.

I think she thought I'd forgotten the conversation. But I hadn't.

I just let it go for a few days until I got everything worked out in my mind, and picked up a few props.

Tonight, as we headed to the bedroom, I told her, generally, what I had in mind, and I had the pleasure of watching her eyes get wide and kind of glazed with anticipation.

Sweet.

Once we got naked, I asked Emily—no, told her—to lie on her back on the bed. She grinned dreamily as she lay down.

Out of my bag of tricks I first pulled a pair of black-leather cuffs. They weren't bondage cuffs, just plain bands with studs like a rocker would wear onstage. I made sure she could see that there was no way to attach them to anything before I buckled them around her wrists.

"My God, you look sexy," I said. "The dark leather against your pale skin. I wish I'd found bigger ones for your ankles."

She lifted her hands and turned her wrists back and forth, admiring the cuffs.

"I didn't say you could do that," I told her. I kept a little teasing note in my voice, figuring we'd lead up to things slowly.

I arranged her like the model in the picture, legs spread wide, a pillow under her ass so her pussy was even more exposed, hands on her thighs.

It was difficult to go slow when she looked so damn hot.

"Don't move," I told her. "The game tonight is you hold still until I say it's okay to move."

She disobeyed immediately with a little squirmy shiver. It was cute and made her breasts jiggle enticingly, but I still shook my head and said, "Bad girl. Just for that, I won't touch you yet."

Instead, I posed at the foot of the bed, took my cock in my own hand, and began to stroke. I was already hard, just from looking at her, from how she allowed me to pose her on the bed, from how she obeyed me now, unmoving except for breathing heavily as she fixed her gaze on my hand.

I thumbed the slick moisture from the tip of my cock and held it to her lips. She started to stick her tongue out, then stopped, remembering.

"Good girl," I said. "You may taste now."

I slipped my finger between her lips. She sucked eagerly, and I felt the sensation all the way down to my cock.

As tempting as it was to encourage her to suck my cock, I resisted. We had a lot more to do before we got to that stage of the game.

Then again, it could all be part of the game.

"You like that, do you?" I asked, pumping my finger in and out of her mouth, just a little. "I'll bet you'd like it even more if I let you suck my cock."

She whimpered, eyes wide.

"You're probably just dying to reach out and take it in your hands, but you can't, because you're not allowed to move." I pulled my hand away from her and slowly stroked my cock a few times for good measure, watching her watch me.

I stopped only because I was getting too excited myself.

Kneeling between her spread legs, I braced my hands on either side of her and leaned down to kiss her. I let only our lips and tongues touch, keeping my body away from her. She'd want to press up, wrap around me for full-body contact, and I thought I felt her tense to do so before she remembered.

When I was satisfied that she was well kissed, I moved down to capture one rosy nipple in my mouth. She gasped with pleasure. I suckled gently, teasing her, not giving her the pressure she really wanted. I blew on the wet flesh, watching it pucker. Emily would have loved to thread her hands through my hair and pull my face against her, encouraging me to bite and twist her nipples, but I held off.

Then Emily asked, "Am I allowed to talk?"

I grinned. "Did I say you were gagged?"

"No."

"Then talking's fine."

"I want you to play with my nipples harder," she said.

"What's the magic word?" I trailed my fingertips across her breasts, circling her areolas.

"Please. Oh, God, please. I can't stand it!"

I did play with them harder, but gradually, working my way up to nibbling and grazing my teeth against one while I pinched and tweaked the other. And I stayed there a good long time. I was giving Emily exactly what she wanted, but to the point that it was getting her so aroused that she was going insane. She was reduced to babbling and imploring me to lick her, to touch her clit, to do something.

I let her beg for a few minutes, because it was turning me on something fierce, before I left a trail of kisses down her abdomen and turned my attention to between her spread thighs. She was so wet, her lips swollen and her clit pouting, I wanted to dive in and lick her, taste her, feel her quiver and hear her scream as I brought her to orgasm again and again.

Instead, I slowly slid one finger into her. Her inner muscles clenched around me, but it wasn't enough to make her come, just drive her a little more crazy. I removed my finger, caressed her gently from pussy to clit to ass, leaving a glistening trail. I slipped inside her again, gave a little teasing crook of my finger, and pulled out to the sound of her hissing breath. I used her own moisture as I played with her anus, just around the opening.

Then I pulled out my next items: a bottle of lube and a string of anal beads.

Her eyes widened.

Coating my fingers, I carefully slid in and out of her, making sure she was relaxed and comfortable before I slid the beads in, one by excruciating one. I swear the hair on her forearms was standing up by the time I was finished.

I tugged on the string, just a little, as she got used to the feeling of the beads stuffed inside her. I swear her clit was twitching. I'd never seen Emily so aroused, so on edge.

Bondage, even only verbally enforced, was very, very good for her.

Finally, I indulged my own desires and bent forward to lick her. I ran my tongue between her lips and all the way around her before flicking lightly against her clit. Her hips twitched, but she kept her butt firmly on the bed, as much as it must have been driving her crazy not to push against the fleeting pressure and find her release.

"You've been very good," I said. "Here's your reward."

I fluttered my tongue against her needy clit and at the same time, as she started to pitch over the edge, I pulled the anal beads from her.

Emily screamed.

Her hands were clenched, her wrists pressed against her thighs as if they were actually trapped there. Her hips rocked up a little, but no more than they would if her ankles had been tethered to the bedposts. Her face contorted, her head thrashed back and forth, and the muscles in her neck stood out in relief from the force of her orgasm and her efforts not to move with it. Just as I'd imagined when we'd talked a few days ago, her hair was a wild tangle around her, and her body glistened with a light coat of sweat.

Gorgeous. Wild and lustful and just plain gorgeous.

My cock ached from want, and after that performance, I saw no need to hold off.

When I thought she might be able to answer a simple question, I asked her, "Do you want me to come in your pussy or your mouth?"

Emily licked her lips. "My mouth. Please."

She twitched, started to sit up. "Hold still," I said. "I'll let you know when you can move."

I shifted position, lifted her head so I could stick a pillow under it. Then I more or less knelt down over her face, stuck my cock into her mouth and began moving it in and out—slowly at first, a tease for both of us. "I'm fucking your mouth tonight," I said. "Hold still and suck. I'll do most of the work."

Keeping the patter up was tough enough with her hot little mouth around me, my cock moving between her lips, feeling the slight tug of her teeth now and then.

But as I started moving faster and she caught the rhythm, sucking harder, caressing me with tongue and lips and pressure as I pushed in and out, talking coherently became out of the question. I was holding back as best I could, trying not to gag her, making myself resist the urge to fuck her mouth as hard and fast as I would her pussy.

It wasn't easy. I was close, so close. I needed just a little more stimulation.

"Move," I growled. "Use your hands…please…"

One hand fluttered up to play with my taut balls, sending waves of sensation that almost pushed me over the edge.

I couldn't see her dip into her dripping sex, but she must have, because the finger suddenly circling my anus was slick with moisture.

She didn't need to press inside. That did it, that sure, delicate touch.

I lost touch with the planet and pretty much everything on it except my dick for a few delicious seconds as I filled her mouth. It was all I could do to crawl a little forward so I didn't actually land on her face when I collapsed.

"May I move?" she asked. I nodded—talking was still beyond me.

"Love you," she muttered. "That was…wow." She squirmed so that, lying more or less on her stomach, she could throw one leg and one arm over me.

She may have said something else, but I couldn't be sure because the next thing I knew it was almost dawn and we were still tangled together, her body holding me immobile as my words had held her.

CHRIS COSTELLO

THE GUY YOUR MOTHER
WARNED YOU ABOUT

"HEY, COULD I GET A HEFEWEISEN over here?" I shouted at the top of my lungs, trying to be heard over the music blaring from the speakers. To me, my voice sounded squeaky, girly, too feminine—but the nasty look I got from Karita told me I was doing fine.

I drew more dirty looks as I waited for my drink, which gave me a thrill. I could practically feel my cock throbbing in my pants as I leered at all the beautiful girls—and I felt like I should be embarrassed for having a hard-on. How long would it take them to make me, I wondered? Longer than I thought, as it turned out, because nobody came over and sat next to me.

Fuck, I thought. *I did it.*

Looked like nobody I knew well had decided to show up that night; that was probably part of the reason nobody spotted me. But I guess I still must have looked pretty convincing to get that kind of negative attention.

Karita was a twentysomething punkette like me, only way more femme than I could ever hope to be (or want to). She was wearing a tight pair of leather pants that laced up the sides and a tight, low-cut, bright-red tank top that said, "I'M THE GUY YOUR MOTHER WARNED YOU ABOUT." It was cut off just below her breasts. She looked even better than usual, and my practiced male swagger made me want to leer at those full breasts, the pretty face and bee-stung lips in a weirdly entitled fashion. I felt as if I had every right to walk up to this distant acquaintance and bury my face between her breasts, just because I wanted to, which was something I had never felt in my life.

Feeling like that was making me incredibly wet.

It was an empty night at the CoCo Club—maybe twenty women lounging about in various stages of festivity, a few of them dressed up, but most in their casual Sunday clothes—jeans, T-shirts, sharkskin jackets, leather, the uniform of mostly-under-thirty San Francisco dykes on the make.

Sexy, tough, rugged, hip.

There in the corner, though, sat the girl of my dreams. She was pale and gorgeous, femme and curvy and more than a little slutty look-ing, an impression she obviously cultivated. She always dressed up—I'd never seen her without heels, makeup, and her hair done up with that messy just-fucked look she liked to work. Tonight the girl was wear-ing a tight little red dress that would have been a slip on a more proper girl, and just barely that. I could see her breasts, braless, and her panty lines through the tight red slip, which my inner lech found incredibly sexy. She was also wearing a red feather boa casually draped around her shoulders, a trademark I'd seen on her more than a few times. Her stockings were black fishnet, the lace tops and garters visible just under the hem of the slip, and she had what must have been four-inch heels—wearing that kind of heels would have given me a broken nose if I was lucky.

Karita had told me her name was Danielle, but we'd never been formally introduced. Still, we'd flirted more than a few times, and how I'd never managed to even get an introduction was beyond me, especially now that I was pumped up on imaginary male hormones. I resolved to walk up to her and introduce myself, then suddenly felt the butterflies in my stomach that had taken me over the last three times I'd tried. It's not like Danielle hadn't given me more than a few smoldering looks, but I was supposed to be the butch here, wasn't I?

Not that I was a real butch, most of the time—oh, I tried for that hard-edged swagger and a sneering chuckle, but a perky, boyish bounce and a red-faced and vaguely unfeminine giggle was the best I'd been able to manage. Tonight was different, though—I wasn't just butch, I was a sexist pig and itinerant male oppressor, so Danielle could bloody well blow me. I'd barely had that thought when I saw her looking at me with a dreamy expression, a smirk on her face—had she made me? Or was she just so impressed by my cojónes in walking in here that she figured I was cool even if I was a party-crashing straight dude?

God, she was fucking gorgeous—big brown eyes and long black hair that contrasted hard against her pale skin, lips painted the color of blood. I wanted to taste those lips so bad it hurt.

Karita took her time with the beer, finally sauntering over well after I'd cracked the *Sports Illustrated* swimsuit issue I'd brought along—

the finishing touch, in case I had failed to piss anyone off. When Karita came over, she told me, much colder than the beer, "Three-fifty."

I handed her a five. "Here you go, doll face," I said in my gruff voice, and patted her ass. "You can keep the change."

That's when she made me—lucky thing, too, because her fist was already balled up. Dykes like Karita don't slap.

She bent forward and peered into my face.

"Trey?" she asked tentatively. Then, "Tracey?"

"The name's Chad," I told her. "That's a great pair of pants you're wearing, honey. Nice top, too. And I like what's in it. You know, I really *am* the guy your mother warned you about. What time do you get off?"

"Oh, I'm getting off right now," she said, smirking at me. "Don't worry, I won't blow your cover, but you're about to get lynched on the dance floor if nobody but me takes a closer look."

I crushed out my cigarette. "Thanks, sweet cheeks," I said, hoping she didn't see me go pale. "You need a big comfortable lap to sit in later, you know where to find me."

"Oh, I'll find you," she grinned. "But I have the feeling Danny's going to find you first."

A chill went down my spine. Some leather fag bouncer they'd hired, maybe?

"Danny?"

"Danielle," said Karita. "Don't tell me you haven't seen the way she's looking at you, *Chad*."

Danielle was staring, her chin propped on her fist, her eyes roving over me from across the bar.

I reddened.

Karita disappeared and I drank half my Hefeweisen in one gulp. I tried to light another Marlboro and found my hands were shaking. I told myself this was too crazy—I couldn't just walk over there and turn on the charm like some tough guy. I couldn't even change the fucking oil on my Kia Sephia, for God's sake. All right, I would have two more beers and then I'd go up and introduce myself to Danielle as Trey, she'd recognize me, I'd take off the mustache, I'd slip off the sharkskin suit and the suspenders, unknot the tie, and take off the dress shirt so she could see my slight breasts in the white undershirt I wore, know it was really me. Then we'd have a laugh over it and maybe I could ask for her phone number, take her to a film festival week after next. That was always good for a first date. No way was I going to play this charade of drag-king swagger with a girl I actually liked—that would be stupid; she'd never go for it. That sort of thing would seem silly to an accomplished glam queen like Danielle.

"Excuse me, sir?"

I looked up from my beer and my ears popped; all of a sudden I felt dizzy and nauseous.

"Y–yes?"

"I don't believe we've been introduced," said Danielle, standing closer to me than I expected—so close I could smell her perfume even over the cigarette smoke and beer and sweat of the bar. What was it? Something I recognized, something my older sister Candace had worn to her junior prom.

"I'm Danielle." She put out her hand, palm down.

I remembered my manners and stood. "I'm Chad," I said, touching my lips to her hand and lingering a bit too long. "Chad Cooper."

I found myself taking a deep breath, sniffing up her arm like some character from a Bugs Bunny cartoon. I turned her hand over and smelled her wrist, finally placing the scent.

"Chanel No. 5," I said. Now *that's* femme. "A beautiful scent for a beautiful woman." My heart was pounding and I felt like I was about to faint—or throw up on her. That wouldn't have been very butch at all.

"Oh, Mr. Cooper," said Danielle, making a show of hiding her face and even blushing a little bit—how the hell did she manage that?—even while her eyes showed a wicked sparkle and she licked her lips sexily. "You're flattering me. I always get so embarrassed when men flatter me!"

"I'm sure it happens a lot," I said. "And please call me Chad."

"Oh, I couldn't," she said. "We've just met. I don't want to seem, you know, *that* way."

"Oh, there's nothing wrong with being that way," I said. "And besides, we're going to get a lot more familiar, you know." Fuck, had I actually said that? Impossible. Feeling drunk with power and fear, I said, "Please sit down."

She moved to sit in the chair across from me, and I gently grasped her arm. "Not there," I said, hardly believing I was doing this. I patted my lap. "It's much more comfortable over here."

"Oh, I couldn't." She managed to suppress the smile that played at the edge of her mouth. I could see her nipples through the thin silk of her slip—harder than before? Was this turning her on? I knew I was so wet I could have slid right out of my chair.

"Please," I said, and Danielle didn't have to be asked a third time. She slid into my lap and draped her arms around my shoulders, her breasts just inches from my face and straining to get through that lacy slip. Playfully, she twined her feather boa around my neck and tickled my nose with the other end. I breathed deeply of her scent and felt my cunt respond, my nipples pressing against the Ace bandage I'd used to bind my breasts. I knew from the way Danielle was sitting that she could feel the bulge of the precariously-arranged dildo strapped to my body and stuffed into my jockstrap—and in case I had any doubts, she began to squirm against it, rubbing her ass against my cock as if casually—but there wasn't anything casual about it.

I looked up into Danielle's gorgeous face, hoping I didn't look too much like a schoolgirl in love. To cover it up, I let one hand fall unceremoniously to the place where her ass rested on my knee, and brought my other hand up to her thigh, placing it where her garters met her lace-top fishnets, right at the lace hem of her slip, so much so that my thumb even went underneath the garment. I smiled up at her mischievously, like an adolescent boy doing something bad, which is how I felt—the part of me that wasn't terrified she'd slug me and my chances would be ruined.

But she didn't slug me, didn't pull away. Instead, she snuggled closer, letting her breasts hover ever closer to my face while she ran her fingers through my hair. She cocked her head and breathed seductively into my ear.

"Waitress," I shouted. "Get this lady a drink!" Then, softer, "What're you drinking, Danielle?"

"Cosmopolitan."

"One cosmopolitan," I shouted to Karita. "You must have watched that HBO show with all those women."

"In bed with my clothes off," said Danielle with a smile. "Every fucking week."

Karita brought the cosmopolitan and another beer, and I held up a ten.

"On the house," said Karita. "Dykes with balls get special consideration."

"Then go buy yourself something lacy, doll face," I said, holding out the ten.

Karita smiled. "Oh, you mean it, Mr. Cooper?" She set down the tray of drinks on an adjacent table and put both her hands on her tits, pushing them together and bending forward until she could pluck the bill away with her cleavage. She did exactly that, and I didn't move the bill to make it any easier for her. A couple of women across the bar hooted and applauded as Karita came away with the bill stuck between her breasts at the slight V of her tank top. I guess by then they'd figured out I wasn't a tourist. Karita bent forward and gave me a kiss on the lips.

"Whore," said Danielle, putting her hand on my cheek. "Get your own man." She kissed me, too, her full lips meeting mine and her slender tongue teasing its way into my mouth as Karita made a snide comment—"That's what I was doing, slut"—and danced away.

Danielle's lips parted with mine and she smiled.

"You don't know what a thrill it is to get a man in here," she cooed. "I mean a *real* man." She squirmed some more against my cock.

"I guess you don't get many guys," I said gruffly. "I mean, in *this* kind of a club."

She giggled, kissed my ear. "Well, you know. The management does sort of discourage it. We never know when a virile guy like yourself might walk in and steal all the femmes away."

"Is that right?"

"Oh, yes. You know how we are. We'll come here, all right, but we're just waiting for the right man to come in, drag us home by the hair, and throw us on the bed. That's what we all want, isn't it? Even if we don't know it."

"Is that what you want?"

She looked into my eyes, her big brown ones seducing me in a way I'd never been seduced before.

I slipped my hand up Danielle's dress. Now I could feel the soft skin of her thigh, and I found myself wondering, noticing that with my other hand I couldn't feel those panty lines that had so turned me on when they showed through her slip. I ran my fingertips over the heart shape of her ass and wondered at their lack.

"I took them off," she whispered into my ear. "I thought you'd like that. I know how a tough guy like you doesn't like to waste time undressing a woman."

Now my head was spinning for real, and I thought I truly might pass out. I tried hard not to blush, but as we sat there and drank our drinks, Danielle's flirting increased a notch and we traded double entendres and brushed our bodies against each other. I got wetter with every sultry caress she gave the back of my neck, with every time she ran her fingers through my hair, with every kiss she planted on my lips. I had come in here planning to bewitch with my arrogance and braggadocio, but now this femme was seducing me with all the subtlety of Marilyn Monroe on Ecstasy. I can't say I minded.

"You ever been with a *real* man?" I asked her in between flirts and kisses, in between letting my hands casually graze her breasts as I held her.

"Oh, I turn them into real men," she said, kissing my forehead.

"Think you could pull that trick with me?" I asked.

"I won't need to," she said. "I can tell that right away."

I still don't remember how we made it from the table at the CoCo Club to the stairway leading up to the street. The four or five drinks probably helped, but I would have taken this girl home if I'd been drinking ginger ale.

I helped Danielle on with her long leather coat, feeling a sadness as I watched her button that gorgeous body away from me like a present wrapped before Christmas—as if I were never going to get a chance to unwrap it.

"I don't live far," she said.

"Good," I told her. "My wife is waiting for me at home."

She giggled and led me up the long staircase into the alley. The truth was that my three roommates were probably waiting up for me and would razz me indefinitely if I came home with a sweet thing like Danielle on my arm.

The second we got out in the alley, though, I found myself seized with a sudden urgency. I glanced around to make sure no one was watching—it was midnight on a Sunday night, and the streets would be empty—then grabbed Danielle and pushed her up against the brick wall behind the Dumpster, kissing her and thrusting my hand under her dress. She really wasn't wearing anything underneath.

"Mr. Cooper, please," she sighed, squirming against me as I touched her smooth pussy. "Someone might see."

"That's the idea," I growled, slipping one finger inside her as I kissed her, as she moaned and wriggled against the brick wall and rubbed her tits against my chest. I couldn't believe how wet she was—probably almost as wet as I was.

The alley was open to the street but fairly hard to see from it. I knew more than a few girls who did things in this alley, but I'd never done it myself. I guess I'd never got drunk enough or horny enough. But any guy named Chad Cooper wouldn't hesitate to take his woman in an alley, right? Well, at least, that was my fantasy.

I slipped my hand out of Danielle's pussy, brought it to my mouth, and licked it. Then she licked it, too, and we kissed hungrily around my finger and the sharp taste of her pussy. I pushed my sharkskin-clad leg up between Danielle's legs and shoved it hard into her crotch. She clamped her thighs around my knee and whimpered. We were in an alley filled with Dumpsters and trash, but all I could smell was Chanel No. 5. I dropped to my knees and slipped both my hands up under Danielle's dress, pulling it almost to her waist, staring hungrily at her meticulously shaved pussy.

I pushed Danielle against the side of the Dumpster, easing her ass up onto the little shelf so she could spread her legs wider, and buried my face between her spread thighs. I slid my tongue between her swollen lips and tasted the sharp tang of her juice, which was dribbling out as fast as I could lap it up. I teased my way up to her clit and suckled it gently into my mouth, flicking my tongue tip violently up and down against it in a quickening rhythm.

"Oh, God," she moaned, and gripped my hair to pull my face harder into her. "More," she whimpered. "Harder. Do it harder."

I sucked as hard as I could and lapped my tongue rhythmically up on her clit, working the tip under the hood so I could get to her most sensitive spot. Every time I did, I was rewarded with a shuddering groan of ecstasy. Both of us no longer cared who saw or heard. I licked faster and Danielle threw her head back. "Don't stop!" she gasped as she grabbed the edge of the Dumpster and lifted both of her legs all the way into the air. "Don't! I'm going to come!"

I brought her over the edge, feeling her thighs closing on my head like a nutcracker and her body twisting atop me as she spasmed. Her feather boa dislodged itself somehow and dropped down around my shoulders, its ends coiling on the ground. Danielle kept moaning, "Fuck me, fuck me, fuck me," as she came, so when I felt the rhythmic convulsions of her body slowing and stopping, I put one hand on her belly to keep her from falling off the Dumpster and pulled myself up with the other. I wedged her against the Dumpster with my body and reached down to unzip my pants.

She stared into my eyes, her face and breasts flushed with orgasm. She had the hungry look of a woman who wants to be fucked so bad she'll die if she doesn't get it in the next ten seconds. I must have taken fifteen or twenty fumbling with my belt and slacks and jockstrap, because she closed her eyes and turned away, sounding like she was sobbing hysterically as she gasped, "Fuck me, fuck me, fuck me!"

Then I had my dick in my hand, and I leaned back to let a long stream of spit dribble onto the head.

"Oh, God," she moaned. "Yeah. Fuck me."

I rubbed the spittle-slick head against Danielle's clit a few times, feeling her body shudder every time I did. Was she too sensitive for that right after coming so hard? I didn't even care. I was going to fuck her the way I wanted to fuck her, and something told me that was exactly what she wanted, too. I teased her mercilessly, making her beg me a dozen times and more.

"Put it in," she whimpered over and over again. "God, please, put it in me. I need your cock."

Then I nuzzled it against the entrance to her cunt and pushed it in, feeling her postclimax tightness clamp hard against my entry. I got it into her and started fucking her, slowly at first, then faster as she begged me.

"Harder," she whispered into my ear. "Fuck me harder, Mr. Cooper. Fuck me like I don't matter. Make yourself come inside me."

So I did, pounding into her as hard as I could, until I heard her moaning again and I knew from the shuddering of her body that she was coming a second time. I threw back my head and made the gruffest, most masculine grunt I could manage, and hissed: "I'm gonna come, baby—I'm gonna come in your pussy!" Then I realized I had no fucking idea what a guy felt like when he came, or what his body moved like, not the faintest clue what I should do when I shot my load in Danielle's pussy. But as if from heaven, my roommate Tony's fag porn came to me in a rush—of barely academic interest when I watched it, mind you, but now I could remember the frenzied motions of the leather boys as they came on each other. I tried to approximate that, shuddering in just that way and thundering, "Oh, yeah!" as I came.

When we ground to a halt, Danielle slumped against me, kissing my neck. "I still don't live far," she told me.

I pulled down her dress, buttoned up my sharkskin slacks, and buckled my belt. Then I led her by the hand away from the Dumpster

I'd just fucked her against. I stopped when I saw Karita leaning up against the doorway to the club, smoking a cigarette.

"I'm sorry," she said, breathing smoke. "You were making so much noise I just couldn't resist. I hope you don't mind?"

I looked at Danielle, who shrugged and smiled. I shrugged, too. Danielle leaned over and gave Karita a quick kiss on the lips. "But you may *not* come home with us—at least not tonight."

Karita laughed nervously, and so did I—a very unmasculine sound. Danielle and I left Karita standing there smoking in the alley and walked the four blocks to Danielle's apartment.

RAKELLE VALENCIA

HEADING AND HEALING

H USH, OR WE'LL HAVE TO HOG-TIE you, too," my wife said.
The rope dug into my Wranglers at the ankles. I was slammed
flat to my back by the horse dragging my feet out from under
me. The Honda snugged my leather boot tops, gouging out a mark
that would have cut deeply into my skin. I shouldn't have stepped
off my horse in such a huff to walk off some aggravation. Practice
stunk, and if my new partner had been a guy, I would have punched
him one in the kisser. Instead, I was fit to be tied with no means of
physical release for my frustrations, and she took advantage of that
by roping me.

Wiggling upright to sit on my ass, I felt the second rope drop
before my hands could reach the first. I knew what they were doing. I
was healed, then headed, so to speak. But I was no damned steer, and
fooling around like this was dangerous, near to getting a fellow torn in

half like those old stories of gladiator times when they quartered folks with four horses for fun or retribution. So I got nervous fast.

Until Kassy, my new header, stepped down from her quarter horse, Spike, and my wife threw me a hint of slack as she dismounted my own roping horse, Dregs. "This ain't funny," I said in a gruff manner that sent the women giggling.

"Hush, or we'll have to hog-tie you, too," my wife replied.

At least they took the ropes down off the saddle horns. Dregs had been known to be a sadistic joker, and I wasn't real confident that he'd stay put once he surmised my position of being stretched out between the two waxed ropes. I wasn't real sure he'd cut me slack instead of making this bad situation worse. He was a rehab that I had picked up along the way and tried to find a job for since no one else was getting along with him proper. He had never attempted to throw me per se, but he was cagey, knowing just how things should go, then doing the opposite unless I knew enough ahead of time to stop him. And the bugger was quick.

With a slight bit of relief, I flopped back into the dirt to lie flat waiting for the giggling twosome to set upon me, most likely with their demand for me to cool off. My wife threw a leg over and squatted above my chest, adjusting her rope from my torso to cinching my wrists. She was my wife, so I let her.

But then Kassy threw a couple of loops and a hooey around my bound ankles with some determination. Now, Kassy was a drifter of sorts. She followed the rodeos. She and Spike could run the speed events, taking most of the buckles every time, but she was a better all-around cowboy than that. Heading steers in the team event with a man healin' was about the only other work she could get, when she could get it. Pro rodeo was still pretty tough on letting the women compete.

I had watched Kassy and invited her back to my ranch as a potential new partner. My last partner had to get his shoulder dislocated for the fourth time, riding bulls. He was now out of the point-running. Which left me out unless I could wrangle a partner this late in the game. There was only Kassy.

My wife licked her lips and threw a couple of loops and a hooey around my wrists, then stood, convincing my arms to stay above my head with her pointed-toed boots pressing into my pits.

My indoor arena was dead quiet except for the snuffling of the two horses as they wandered away toward a bale of hay used as a practice roping dummy for my three-year-old kid who was now fast asleep under the watchful eye of his grandmother up in the old house.

"Hon?" I asked. I knew I had been acting a little hot under the collar with Kassy since there was a lot riding on those earned points. I also knew my wife had taken her side of things and had asked me to lighten up. But I couldn't. And I knew that I had gotten unbearable. My tension was seething to boiling. "Hon?" I repeated more tentatively.

In reply, she tugged at her gritty zipper, surprising me with nothing on under those taut Wranglers. She shimmied out of them, kicking her boots off at the same time and stood half naked above me with her crinkly, pruned triangle of hair taunting my sight.

I said no more. That is, until I heard my belt pop open like a soda can and my own zipper complain of being yanked, hard. "What…what's going on?" I panicked. Tried to kick at Kassy until my wife dropped down to hover over me.

She tore at the pearly snaps of her Twenty-X shirt and leaned on all fours, positioning to fill my mouth with a pert, red nipple while reaching above my head to pressure my tied wrists deeper into the sand. I suckled, forgetting Kassy at that moment.

Kassy walked up and kissed my wife. I'm not talking a small, innocent peck to the lips—it was hot! She grabbed my wife's hair, entangling fingers, to pull her head upward, then teased her with an open mouth, gently touching my wife's bottom lip with the tip of her pink tongue just to move away and start again.

The wife's nipple slipped from my open lips as I gawked. My cock grew in my boxer shorts, and I was glad for the relief Kassy had afforded me before this new torture began.

Their eyes made contact and never left as their mouths danced in an erotic tease. Finally, Kassy sucked my wife's bottom lip into her mouth and tempted their tongues into play. A feminine hand lifted the weight of my wife's breasts, fondling them, pulling at each nipple and twisting them to my wife's muffled moans and groans. The hand that had been wrapped in long brunette tresses eased away to where I could only imagine.

I licked my own lips and looked toward my wife's pussy, seeing thin, rugged fingers circling her clit shaft. Those fingers drew back, following the crack of ass, and ending, I believed, by my wife's lower lumbar because that palm had urged her to sit up and forward, fully on my face, leaving my tied hands alone in the trade for balance.

Kassy gave one last kiss to my wife before I felt those same lips at the tip of my cock's head that had poked its way from cotton captivity. She fisted my shaft, moving the skin up and down its length as her tongue swirled the head and poked into my piss-slit.

My legs kicked once or twice. My mouth hummed with words that were never heard. And my wife began to rock harder on my lips, her engorged clit shaft hitting the tip of my nose, juices sluicing the sides of my stubbly face. I stuck my tongue out and did my best to stroke her hole, which wasn't easy with the rocking force of an entire body sitting square on my mug.

I dragged the thirty-foot rope by tied wrists to reach for those beautiful breasts. Their heft swayed in my calloused hands until I could find and pluck at the nipples one at a time. Incoherent sounds gurgled in my wife's throat. And I knew, somewhere in the back of my thick skull, that she was close to orgasm.

But my dick was in Kassy's mouth. I'm a guy, and I can vouch for the fact that the little head does take over the thinking for the big head at times. This was definitely one of those times. With sweet pussy on my lips, I still couldn't help but think only of the velvet sheath that swathed my prick.

My tied legs no longer jerked, but my hips bucked. I beat a rhythm into that deep throat until my balls crimped up to where they were almost nonexistent outside of the body. I twitched. I lunged. I moved this side, then that. Kassy rode to stay with it, just like at the pro rodeos.

My wife popped off first. I only realized it when she bore down so hard as to sore up my jaw and slop me to soaking by squirting. I tried to get my mind to her. I tried to rub her breasts just how she liked, though I was hampered by waxed rope tied tightly about my wrists and my brain losing any type of focus other than toward my groin.

Kassy's calloused fingers took over for her warm mouth, easing the need to shoot my load immediately. She went back to seductively kissing my wife as her other hand lay flat between those breasts, urging my wife off my face and aiding in impaling that sopping, spasming twat onto my cock.

I lost it. I shot load after load while watching my new arena partner seducing my wife with her passionate kissing.

The horses had made short work of the bale and now snuffled the sodden, sandy tangled mess of human flesh, sturdy cotton work clothes, and waxed ropes. Kassy got up and led the animals away by their bits. "I think I'll let them cool down," she said as she exited the indoor arena.

I didn't know whether she meant the horses or my wife and me. But it didn't matter, I was healed and headed and laid out like a good-scoring steer. I let the ropes have me then. There was no fight left in my bondage.

SHANE ALLISON

FLAT-FOOTED

HATE WHEN PEOPLE TAP ME on the shoulder. Don't like to be bothered. 'Specially by people I don't care for anyway. Wish that I could say that I was happy to see David, but I wasn't. Wasn't in the mood to be watched by this guy who gets off watching others get off. Fucking perv. I was having one of my bad days. One of those days where nothing was going right.

David picked the worst time to come around here, bugging me, tapping me on my shoulder of self-loathing. He took a seat next to me, asked how I was doing, wanted to know how things were going. "Fine," I said. I haven't heard from the bastard in weeks. Hate when people ask how I'm doing. My mouth was just too lazy to speak that day. I just wanted to punch him in the face. I hated everyone in the world, despised everything on this planet. I couldn't have been in a shittier mood.

David asked me if I wanted to mess around. I knew what he meant. I sensed what he was after. I needed a break from doing absolutely nothing, from spending all that time wasting time. We couldn't say much, couldn't talk too loud with this guy cuter than David sitting next to us with papers and index cards strewn. I grabbed my bag and followed him. I stared hard at the back of his head grown with salt-and-pepper waves of hair. I would have burned a hole clean through his breeder skull if I had the Superman means to do so. Like I said, he picked the wrong damn day to screw with me, to come lusting after me like some hound in heat. But that's what he wanted, so I gave it to him. Goddamn weirdo. We sneaked into the only men's room that was on this floor, the same stall from the last time we did this, the only one that was big enough to hold what we were about to do. Hung my bag on the coat hook screwed to the back of the stall door. I watched David unbuckle his belt, unfasten himself out of dirty jeans. He's a maintenance worker over at the civic center, you see, so that's why he's so filthy. He sat upon the commode with thighs ajar, thick with waves of black fur. His red shirt that had his name embroidered in yellow letters was hiked above the belly button. His dick was no bigger than a circus peanut. He looked up into my face and smiled, showing off those perfect, Fixodent dentures. He sat there leaning against those hard toilet pipes. He's such the freak. I worked my feet out of the black Polo flip-flops. You should have seen the way he pawed at them last time, the way he took my socks and inhaled what had been held hostage in shoes all day. Last week, he buffed my toes with his tongue to a high shine.

David and I met through a Craigslist ad. Said he was looking for someone whose toes he could suck, whose arches and heels he could worship like gods. Answered his ad 'cause I was all too familiar with dudes like David. Encountered a few when I was living in New York. Some were into athletic sneaks, while others preferred the insides of blue-collar boots. David preferred me bare, dry, and calloused.

The first guy I encountered that was into feet I met in a basement of a bookstore on Christopher Street that wasn't a bookstore at all, but a place where gay porn was sold, where sex toys lined the walls. I didn't frequent the shop for porno pricks and plastic dildos but for what awaited me just on the other side of the turnstile, just down a set of stairs. Thursdays and Sundays were my nights. For just ten bucks I could have all the dick I wanted. I descended into the basement with booths filled with men fucking and sucking behind wooden doors, men leaning against the wall fondling their dicks in denim all under the watchful eyes of security cameras and Jay Leno cracking jokes under a cloak of TV static. Men of all types, geezers and gods with booze in their eyes, drunk off poppers. Men very different from the mere puppies of Tallahassee. I was a few pounds lighter than I am now. Surviving only on tap water and bologna sandwiches will do that to you. You should have seen the way they were after my ass, staring at my bulge, like the dude I met on that fateful Sunday night. Brawny, tan around the shoulders while he was pale as hell in other areas. He was balding with a storm-gray beard. I stood there shy at the back of the basement, observing those boys sneaking in and out of booths with cum on their trousers, walking out with used rubbers stuck to the bottoms of their shoes.

I gawked at him like the mere piece of trade he was. We played with our dicks through denim and sweats. We wouldn't stop staring. It was like he was trying to see through my nasty little soul. Weren't too many that I was interested in 'cause most of them I already had had in some way, shape, or uncompromising form. Picked them off in my head: *Sucked him off last night, fucked him last week.* Hadn't seen him around those parts of the West Side. Cut through his gaze as he walked around, hard. Had only two hours to spare. They closed at two on Sundays. Was the last call for cock, so to speak. I returned his stare with one of my own. When I yanked at my erection, it caught the eyes of all the guys that had been after me that night. A vacant booth was sandwiched between us. Figured it wouldn't be empty for long if we didn't take advantage right that second. I crept within its insides. The door barely hung on its hinges as I left it cracked to let him know that he was welcome. The booth was one of the bigger ones in the basement, so it was large enough for two randy guys like us. Two men wrestling played out on the monitor before us. The screen was smudged with God knows what. As we both started to strip out of our tees and cut-off sweats, the scent of amyl nitrate filled our lungs.

"Put away those poppers," yelled one of the guards. I was so much of a regular that the smell had no effect on me. Tried poppers once, and they only ended up giving me a headache. I pulled my dick over elastic to show him my goods. His dick wasn't too shabby. We watched each other as we whacked our cocks in unison. There was a concrete slab in our booth, long enough for a body. He lay there nude, jacking his sex that hung out of the cotton panel of his briefs. I felt silly standing there, the two of us massaging our hung dicks. Watched his lips move just slightly. Couldn't make out his words for shit. I moved down and put my ear to the ground to make out his sounds. He looked so helpless. He mentioned something about smelling my feet, about sucking my toes. Thought his command was quite unorthodox but interesting. Kicked off my shoes, exposing dirty flat-footedness I inherited from my Aunt Earline on my dad's side. My socks were black at the bottom. Held up my leg to show him my feet, my archless thirteens. Took his hand and placed it flat against it. He tugged and held my sweaty foot at his face. He jacked off as he breathed in the odor of soiled socks.

Damn, I thought, *the things these guys are into.*

I never felt more ridiculous than with myself hiked up on that anonymous face, his nose grazing along the backs of my toes.

"Too bad you're wearing socks," he whispered.

I told him he could take them off, which he wasted no time doing, tossing the socks asunder in order to give more attention to my feet. His lips felt sweet as he kissed my feet. I watched his tongue slither in and out of the grooves of plump piggies. Grimaced darkly as he sucked and slurped at toenails, as he beat off searching my face for a response to his filthy act. He bit at my meaty heels, gnawed on my toes like a disobedient puppy. He inhaled my soles like they were bottles of Rush. I watched as his dick grew harder with every sniff, with every toe that he took into his bearded mouth. We ended the night with him coming all over himself. Semen staining faded jeans. We went our separate ways with the aftermath of my feet on his tongue. I dismissed myself upstairs to a booth where I beat off to some cheesy porn movie.

David reminded me of that bearded guy. It's the way he liked lapping at my toes, sucking away. I pressed my socked foot against his chest grown with snow-white fur that felt rough against the flatness of my soles. My dick was stiff, but not enough for David to notice. He kissed the big toe, licked along the thick, hearty part of it. He searched my face but I had no expression to give. I could've kicked him in the face if I wanted. I'd had such a day of it. David looked so stupid sitting there with my foot in his mouth. Damn freak. He worked on the other toes. Got my whole foot wet with spit, but I didn't care. We all have our vices. David made an attempt to fit all my toes in. Man was crazy. I held on to the top of the paper-towel dispenser and the metal railing as I forced my toes in his mouth. I talked dirty to him—told him to take it, to eat my toes. His face was a swell shade of blush; tears welled up in those hazel eyes. Felt guilty, like I was hurting David, so I slowly pulled out of his big mouth. I used my toes to fidget with his nipples. He liked it when I did that. My legs were becoming a four-alarm fire, so we switched positions. I sat upon the throne of the commode while he was on bended knee. Ran my foot along his aging face. I worked the other out of the flip-flop. He pressed his mug into my feet, licking at all ten of my piggies. I once thought I had a thing for feet, but that lasted all of two minutes when I couldn't get past the dude's hairy toes. The mischievous part of me wanted to make David bleed, but the angel won over the devil, and I fed him my toes with gentle ease. He got them good and wet like last time. Lapped at them like a back-alley mutt. His tongue tickled like you would not believe. Took everything in me not to laugh. I looked down as he worked his dick between his thighs. All that white pubic hair along the groin. David never looked hotter than with my feet in his mouth. Nothing was going right for me that day. Nothing except for that. Fucked his face with my size thirteens. A far cry from my well-endowed norm I would have preferred him to lick and suck upon. I wanted him to come for me. He liked me most when I would tell him what to do. Goddamn masochist.

"Faster," I told him. I didn't have all day. Dirty little monkey. I looked at him and thought of bad poppers, men wrestling, and Jay Leno. He grunted as he came. Sweat trickled along his face. I pulled my feet out of his mouth and pushed him naked and spent against the stall wall that was defaced with gang insignia. Held my feet beneath the faucet and rinsed them clean of David's aftermath. I worked them back into my flip-flops, grabbed my bag and sauntered out into the lobby, leaving David drained and naked on the basement bathroom floor. Yeah, he picked the wrong day that day, bothering someone who didn't want to be bothered.

TeReSa NOeLLe ROBeRTS

On a Knife Edge

HONED STEEL SURROUNDED ME, and the sharp tang of the oil used to protect carbon steel filled my nostrils as I walked in the door of Anderson's Artisan Knives. Located in an out-of-the way corner of a neighborhood filled with galleries and high-end artisans' shops, the store—long and skinny and about the size of a good-sized closet—was quite unlike any place I'd been before in my quest for the perfect knife. None of the familiar Henckels and Wüsthof found in kitchen stores—not that I didn't love the heft and balance of my ten-inch Henckels professional chef's knife or the substantial feel of my Chinese cleaver, for culinary purposes, but they were mass-produced, impersonal. None of the same-old, same-old hunting knives and pocket knives I'd seen in half a dozen Army-Navy stores—perfectly good blades, useful for any number of purposes, but soulless.

The knives here were art. Real art, not like the stupid "art knives" made to appeal to people's inner teenage boys, with crap blades that won't take an edge and pretty handles in the form of dragons or naked women that don't actually fit your hand. No, these were exquisite, like something you'd see in a museum: not overly decorated, but a perfect fusion of form and function.

Knives with elaborately incised but functional bone handles, or handles of richly grained wood, clean lined and unadorned and perfect in their simplicity.

Knives tiny enough to hide in your palm.

Knives that were almost swords.

Knives that looked like they belonged in a museum, with a label something along the lines of *Fifth century. Found in bog in Denmark with apparent human sacrifice.*

Carbon-steel blades, dark and, in some cases, clearly handmade, the marks of the forge and the hammer apparent on them.

My mind buzzed with questions, but the proprietor was nowhere to be seen.

I wandered from display case to display case, all but salivating over the wares. My heart was beating faster than normal. My palms were sweating.

And my palms weren't all that was damp. All that steel was getting to me.

My fascination with knives has never been purely that of a collector. In the presence of a well-made knife with a sharp, well-honed blade, I can't help imagining its cold kiss on my skin. First a caress, a mere brush with the flatside—running over my nipples and bringing them to instant, hard arousal. Then a tease, no pain, but that edge of anticipation, of pleasurable fear, as the sharp edge passes lightly over the surface of my skin, trailing goose bumps and ecstasy behind it.

Then comes the cutting. My skin parting behind it. The brief lapse between cut and pain you get with a truly sharp knife. The bright jeweled blood, not a fountain or a gush, but a fine, delicate tracery welling from the cut, beautiful as rubies.

Not that I've done this, not deliberately anyway, and cutting myself by accident just stings (although I admit the time I cut myself in the kitchen with a very sharp Henckels and didn't notice until I saw blood dripping onto the carrots had a hallucinatory fascination). The fantasy involves someone else doing it, occasionally varied with me doing it to someone else. In either case, he's faceless but the knife isn't. Its details vary somewhat, but it's always exquisite.

And very like the knife I was looking at now, with its knotwork-carved bone handle and its slightly curved, very functional blade. It was fairly small, scaled well for my hand, and I could imagine it in the hand of some Viking woman, who'd use it during the day to cut meat or leather….

And at night to mark her man so he wouldn't forget her while he was off raiding Ireland or something. Then he'd return the favor, although maybe he'd use the matching knife, larger-bladed and scaled for a man's hand, in the case next to it.

Runes marked into soft flesh. Marks of possession and passion, made with a beautiful knife.

My knees weakened, my cunt throbbed, and I had to lean against the counter to steady myself.

And a Viking god emerged from a back room.

Did I say "god," generic?

I mean Loki, the trickster, the seducer, the most capricious and dangerous of the Norse pantheon. The long reddish hair, the twinkle in his blue eyes that could equally well be called roguish or sadistic, the mischief in his ruggedly planed face, a face that wasn't conventionally handsome but caught my attention more than if it had been. Trouble was written all over him. Might be fun trouble, might be dangerous trouble.

Might, if I were lucky, be both.

Not that I was likely to find out for real, but I couldn't help thinking that the faceless man in my knife-edge fantasies had found a face.

"May I help you?" he asked. A trace of Scandinavia burred his voice, and my knees went even weaker.

"I'm looking for a very special knife." I managed not to squeak as I said it, but it wasn't exactly a helpful answer. Of course I was looking for a special knife—why else would I be in his shop?

"All my knives are special in some way. Some I've made myself. Others are from other artisans, some American, some Swedish, Norwegian, German. For what purpose do you want this blade?" His voice was gentle, with a hint of tolerant amusement, but something in his eyes, his smile, told me that he knew—*knew*—what I wanted. And liked it.

Hot man, cold steel, hot blood trickling....

No, he couldn't know. No way.

But what if he did?

I had to take the chance. It wasn't as though knife fetishists lurked in every bush.

I took a deep, steadying breath, tried to imagine that Viking woman with her well-honed little blade. She'd say what she wanted, woman to man, unafraid and blunt.

"For cutting," I said, then realized I was stating the obvious yet saying nothing. "Cutting flesh."

"Cooking? Field-dressing game?" A little cock of his head suggested he knew I was prevaricating.

Another deep breath. "Living flesh. Human flesh."

His expression darkened. Still his eyes were bright, but with his face so stern and serious, it was a dangerous light, perhaps sadistic, perhaps a little crazy.

Crazy in the same way I was?

"Are you a cutter? Suicidal?" He loomed over the counter at me and I realized how big he was. Not broad or bulky but tall and hard-bodied, someone who could be a dancer or a danger. Loki for sure. "Get out. Get help or get an ordinary knife, but don't use my blades for your self-destruction." He turned from me, started to walk away.

His backside in jeans was beautiful. His arms were beautiful. I could imagine him looming over me, holding me down as he cut me.

"Wait," I said, caught him before he disappeared into the back. "It's not like that. I…. Knives turn me on. And I want one special blade." The words came out in a shaky rush.

He turned again, smiled at me this time. "For a special someone?" Something about the play of light and shadow there in the back corner made him both glorious and diabolical. Loki indeed, plotting some clever but potentially dreadful mischief.

I wasn't sure where I found the words, let alone the nerve to speak. "For when I find that special someone. I like to be prepared."

"Then you should try out a few, or have them tried out on you, if that's your preference. And I think it is."

Before I could answer, he swept past me—I swear he left wind in his wake—turned his sign from open to closed, pulled a curtain across the inside of the small, barred display window to mask the shop's interior.

Two steps and he was pinioning me to his body, holding my arms at my sides. He smelled like steel—a sharp, cold smell—and leather and smoke and a workingman's sweat, as if maybe he'd been bent over a forge earlier. He kissed like a wolf would, both rough and tender, devouring and devout, as if he wanted to gobble me up whole but wanted even more to make sure there was some of me left for later.

I should have been frightened: a complete stranger whose air of danger was very much part of his attraction, and a shop full of weapons, and things moving much too quickly in a direction that, no matter how much I craved it in my fantasies, yearned for it on the surface of my skin, was potentially deadly.

Instead, it acted like gasoline on the cold fire that steel always sets in me.

Maybe I was frightened, deep down where I wasn't paying attention, but the roiling in my stomach, the shaking hands, the racing heart felt more like arousal than terror, and I leaned into him, opened my lips for him, went at him with tongue and teeth myself, a she-wolf who'd finally found her mate.

His hands were calloused and a little dirty—slurry from sharpening blades, perhaps—but when he caressed my face and down my throat, tracing the line of the jugular vein, I moaned deep in my throat, imagining the same delicate touch from a knife, just skimming my skin, hinting at a million possible deaths without doing any harm. I arched against him.

"Don't move," he said in that Nordic voice, and the hand that had touched my face withdrew. I closed my eyes, then opened them again. I wanted to see.

The knife he unsheathed from his belt was a simple one, utilitarian but elegant in its simplicity, with a dark wooden handle and a blade perhaps three inches long, which, at the moment, looked utterly huge.

I followed it with my eyes as he raised it to the hollow at the base of my throat, the point resting not so much on the surface of my skin as just above it. I could sense the steel radiating energy, but I couldn't feel actual pressure.

I held my breath as he left the knife poised there. Kept holding it as he carefully raised it and with the same delicacy, traced down my cheek, applying no pressure at all, just a whisper of passage. Kept holding it as he moved down the side of my throat, applying just the faintest hint of metallic pressure in the spot where Dracula would like to bite.

I wanted to lean into the blade, but some vestige of common sense—or maybe it was the grip he had on me with his other hand—kept me still.

At least some of me was still. I didn't move or even breathe, but my pussy was twitching and trembling and leaking hot juices that filled my underwear. Close to orgasm already. "Please," I mouthed, afraid—and yet eager—to take the breath I'd need in order to make noise.

"Patience." His eyes twinkled in that evil way, and instead of nicking the tender skin, he withdrew the blade, sheathed it. Then his grin broadened and he grabbed for my crotch, a bold move that I couldn't protest. Not when I writhed against that firm hand like I did, wishing my jeans weren't in the way.

He chuckled. "I can feel how wet you are, right through your jeans. I bet I could make you come right now, on my hand."

I moaned in response, bucked against him.

"But I'm not going to," he said, still rubbing me as if to belie his words. "I could smell it on you, you know, smell how turned on you were by the knives. Told myself it was my imagination, wishful thinking or something. But I was right, I wasn't I?"

I nodded frantically.

"Yeah, I could make you come like this…but what a waste."

With a *shhh* of steel moving against leather, he unsheathed his belt knife again, pressed it against my mound.

Even through denim, I imagined I could feel its cold kiss. I could definitely feel the pressure, the threat—felt it cut straight into my clit and send me flying higher. My eyes widened. I strained, so close to coming I could taste it, willing him to move the blade, to apply just a little more pressure.

"But this isn't really how you want to come, is it? You want to feel it against your skin, feel it cutting you?"

I mouthed, "Yes."

"Then show me which knife you want to feel first."

Trembling, I pointed out the ones that had particularly caught my eye.

"Loki and Sigyn," he said. "They don't all have names but they told me theirs. Sigyn is the wife of Loki in Norse mythology—devoted, but had a few tricks of her own—and I can see from your face you know who Loki is."

I had chosen well.

We ended up in the back room of the shop, set up as a workshop. No actual forge, to my disappointment (but where would it have fit?) but a workbench scattered with tools, dusted with bits of wood, bone, and leather. He moved aside a work in progress—it looked as though he was creating a hilt with a piece of amber inlaid in the pommel—to make room for me to perch on the workbench.

I was hoping he'd simply cut my clothing away, but he didn't. Not until I got down to my bra and drenched, useless panties.

Then with one shudder-inducing flick of lethal little Sigyn on each, he severed my bra straps. The knife, cutting edge out, then traced a path between my breasts, and I had to force myself to hold still at the sweet metal caress. Another flick and the bra fell off, destroyed.

Just as neatly and easily, he cut through the narrow bands of elastic that held my string bikini panties in place. I barely felt the knife touch me—he was that quick and that careful—but it didn't matter. I was lost and I liked it that way.

He changed knives then, switching to Loki, and circled the flat of the blade on one excited nipple. "Please," I whispered, and he knew what I wanted, because he turned the knife, let me taste the edge dancing lightly on that sensitive nub.

The tip pricked the tender nipple once, twice, before he moved on to the other one, torturing me with all too gentle sensation.

"Please." Desperation edged my voice, gave me a blade of my own. "Please, I want to feel…"

He smirked. "Of course you do."

The blade moved down my belly, leaving shudders and a fine white scratch in its wake. The steel was cool, but it set me on fire, and when it reached the curve of my pubic mound, it was all I could do not to buck forward, to provoke him to cut me in that intimate area.

With his free hand, he pushed my knees open. I spread them wider still, wet and yet terrified by a sudden image of him pushing the blade inside me, fucking me with deadly intent.

I clenched and squirmed back at the same time, the seduction of the fantasy warring with its dangerous reality, and with the crazy fact I was playing dangerous games with someone whose name I didn't know.

"Relax," he said, and his deep voice was soothing. "No cuts here. Nothing to mar this pretty pussy. Just a little tease." He turned the knife in his hand, making sure the unsharpened spine was touching me. I saw him do it—but what my eyes told me, my brain and nerve endings refused to accept. The touch of cold steel seared my labia, pierced my clit, brought me to the verge of orgasm. It felt like my skin blossomed with blood behind the knife, but it was only my own juices blossoming in my terrified excitement.

Finally, when I could feel my muscles clenching and jumping, not just in my pussy but all over, so my skin twitched like a nervous race-horse's, he pricked at my mound with the knife while his thumb circled my clit and I rode the warring sensations—cold, hardness, near-pain, and the more familiar spiraling pleasure—to an orgasm that felt like I'd been born into a forge's heat.

When I recovered breath and strength, he asked me, with an old-world gallantry that surprised me under the circumstances, if I were ready for Sigyn to taste me. Something in his manner told me he half-expected a no.

Part of me—the sensible part, I suppose—clamored to say no. But with my pussy drenched and throbbing, my skin still tingling from Loki's gentlest caresses, I couldn't turn back.

He had me lie facedown on the workbench, a worn gray sweatshirt under my head as a pillow.

Panic washed over me when he stepped away, opened a drawer in the workbench. Was he going to pull out a different knife, a larger one, take this fantasy to its bloody, demented conclusion? What sense I had left told me to bolt, but I couldn't move. My body was both languid and tense with anticipation, and I couldn't get it to obey logic. I could barely make myself turn my head to watch him.

What he took out, instead of the cleaver or chain saw my panic told me to expect, was a first-aid kit. He cleaned Sigyn's blade with alcohol, then poured some onto a cotton ball, swabbed at my left buttock, making me clench and curse at the shock of wet chill. Fussed over the area for a while longer.

When he deemed it ready, he let the blade rest against the skin of my ass, pressing in a little. I could tell how sharp it was because, as he moved it, cutting in lightly, it didn't exactly hurt. Not as it passed. There was a fine line of sensation, a combination of cold and heat but not really pain. He moved the blade, cut again.

And only as the skin opened up behind the second cut did I really feel the fire of the first one, sharp and exquisite. It wasn't until the third one that I started to feel hot trickles of blood.

I tightened, imagined what my ass must look like, decorated with fine cuts—was he carving a rune? I felt myself building for another orgasm. My pussy squeezed on nothing, imagined squeezing on the big knife called Loki.

I didn't actually come again, though, until he showed me the blade and the tiny rubies of my blood on it.

He deemed I was shaking too hard to try knife-play on him, but when he stripped down, I could see the scars on him—runes and designs and random patterns—and I knew my chance would come to test Sigyn on his body.

He fucked me from behind, the knife called Loki against my throat and the fact I was pretty sure I'd seen him sheathe it didn't matter much in the state I was in. Not with his cock pounding into me and each thrust jarring the cuts on my ass, making me bleed a little, reminding me of Sigyn's kiss.

He came as if he were stabbing me in the heart through my pussy.

Only when we were spent and trying, listlessly, to clean each other up in the tiny bathroom did I think to tell him my name and ask his.

"Bjorn Anderson," he said, "but my friends call me Loki."

MICHAEL HEMMINGSON

THE END OF CELIBACY

HANNAH HAD A QUIRKY LOOK to her I found appealing—thick, dark-rimmed glasses; a white streak in her otherwise jet-black hair; an odd assortment of attire, cool in this age of the awkward. She was one of the regulars who hung out at the pub down the street from my apartment. Some friends were playing pool, which wasn't my thing. Hannah bought a pitcher of beer and we sat together.

A guy was bending, ready to take a shot at the table, his rear end very close to us. "Get your butt somewhere else," Hannah said, "or I'll take a pool stick and shove it up—"

"That's not very nice," I said. "How'd you like it if someone stuck a pool stick in your ass?"

Hannah raised her brows. "I just might like it."

That was the first clue I didn't get—I wasn't paying attention. I'd recall it in hindsight, yes, as well as overhearing her talk about how her favorite scene in *Last Tango in Paris* was when Marlon Brando put butter up his young lover's back door before sodomizing her.

Soon the beer was gone.

"What will you do now?" Hannah said.

"Don't know," I said.

She took her glasses off and looked at them. "I live a block away, you know."

"No," I said, "I didn't know. So do I."

This was the second clue—and I wasn't paying attention.

"Well," she said.

"Maybe we can go there," I said.

She put her glasses back on. "Okay."

We walked up the block to her place, a small cottage. It was nice, a little messy. I asked how much she paid for it.

"Nothing," she said. "My parents own the property."

"Nice."

"I have beer, I think," she said, going to the kitchen.

I sat on the couch in the small living room.

Hannah returned with two Budweisers. "Yes, I have beer."

She sat next to me.

I don't remember what we talked about. On the floor, I noticed an action figure of the Warner Brothers Martian from the Bugs Bunny cartoon. "I always loved that Martian," I said.

"Me, too," she said, going to the floor and picking it up. "Marvin the Martian. *'I'm going to destroy planet Earth!'* " I touched her hair. She put her head in my lap. It was nice to touch somebody.

"I, um, I don't know what to do," I said.

"What?"

"I haven't been with anyone in a while."

"I don't believe that."

"It's true."

"It's a line," she said. "Do you like me?"

"Yes," I said.

"I like you." She got on the couch with me and we began to kiss. She had to take her glasses off; they were getting in the way. We kissed for a long time. She pushed me back on the couch and lay on top of me. I grabbed her ass, put my hands down her skirt.

She pulled her mouth from mine. "*Bad* boy," she said.

I grabbed her head, and we kissed more.

When I tried to touch her cunt, she stopped me.

"No," she said.

"Sorry," I said.

"Don't worry about it," she said and we kissed.

When I touched her breasts over the fabric of her blouse, she pushed them away. "No, no," she said.

"Sorry," I said.

She took one of my hands and put it back on her ass. "Play with that."

I did and we kissed. My hand and my second hand were all over her butt.

"Hey," Hannah said, "rub my asshole."

"What?"

"With your finger," she said, and I found her asshole with my finger. "In small circles," she said, "yeah, like that—"

She pulled away from me, and sat. She put her glasses on.

"What's wrong?" I asked, moving to her, wanting to kiss her more.

"Nothing," she said. "I have to pee."

"Hey." I grabbed her hand as she stood up. "Can I watch?"

"You want to watch me pee?"

"Yes," I said.

"I need a commitment before I go that far," she said.

"We hardly know each other."

"*Exactly,*" she said, and went to the bathroom.

I sat there.

I got up and followed. The door was unlocked and I went in. Hannah was sitting on the toilet; she glanced up at me. She smiled and said, "You." I could hear the stream of her urine. I sat on the floor, cross-legged.

"You're bold," she said.

"The door was unlocked."

"There *is* no lock."

"I couldn't resist."

She stood up. "Okay, Mr. Bold. Clean me."

"With my mouth?"

"*Ab*solutely not."

I would've done it with my mouth, if she'd asked. I took a wad of toilet paper and wiped her cunt. She pulled her panties up.

"I have to go, too," I said.

"Then I get to watch," she said. "Quid pro quo."

She took my place on the floor; I stood in front of the toilet, took my cock out.

Hannah made a weird sound. She moved, snagged my cock, and put her mouth before it, drinking my urine; what she didn't get flowed out, down her chin, and into the bowl. I liked the sound this made. I breathed hard; it was an experience in itself watching her drink from me.

She pressed her face to my leg. "I'm sorry. I couldn't help myself," she said, softly. "Now you know my fetish. Okay, I'm weird. You'll never love me."

"I could love you," I said.

"Do you mean that?"

"Yes."

"Will you kiss me to prove it?" she asked.

"Yes," I said.

She stood, and we kissed, and I tasted her—and me.

"I want to make love to you," I said.

"No, I can't," she said.

Hannah left the bathroom and sat on the edge of her bed. I sat next to her; we both fell back. It was a nice, big, comfortable bed, the kind of bed I liked, the kind of bed I didn't have.

"It's late," she said, moving away from me. "I'm a little drunk."

"Me, too," I said.

"You can stay here," she said, "if you want."

"I'd like that."

"I'd like it too," she said, standing. "I'm going to turn the light off."

"Okay."

In the dark, I saw her silhouette; she was removing her clothes. I also took my clothes off and got under the covers. She joined me; we didn't touch. My hand went to her body; she was still wearing her bra and panties. I moved closer to her, kissed her.

— 111 —

"I don't think I want to screw," she said.

"Okay," I said.

"I mean, I'm not sure if I can."

"Okay."

"I'm not sure if I'm in the right frame of mind."

"Okay."

"It's not *okay*," she said. "You don't understand, you don't know."

"I *want* to," I said.

"I know you do."

"Hannah," I said.

"It's nice having you in my bed," she said.

"It's nice to be in a bed with someone." She placed her head on my chest and then a hand, playing with the hair. We were quiet, touching each other. Her hand moved down and grasped my cock.

"This is nice," she said.

"Yes," I said, "it is."

"Nice...."

I kissed her on the head.

"I'm twenty-eight years old," she said.

"Yeah?"

"I'm still a virgin."

I laughed, after a moment.

"This is true," she said.

"Now *who* is giving *who* a line?"

She let go of my cock. "I made up my mind years ago that I would save myself for my husband, because some day I plan to marry a nice man. And this man will expect me to be a virgin."

"I see."

"No, you don't see," she said. "I don't expect you to understand. Other men haven't. Like I said, I'm twenty-eight. This doesn't mean I'm not sexual. *Obviously I'm sexual, and I have fetishes.* I'm really pretty basic in that matter—I have a pee fetish, and a butt, you know. I mean, I'm a virgin, *vaginally,* but I like having sex in my butt."

I didn't know what to say.

"I'm terribly attracted to you," she went on. "I want you. I want you inside me. But I want more than a fuck-buddy. I had a fuck-buddy for a while, for a few months. It was just sex, nothing more. I didn't like it. I mean, it was okay but it wasn't me. It was a different me."

"He fucked you in the ass?"

"Yes. I don't know if he liked it that much. Some men do, some don't."

I'd only had anal sex with a woman once, and I think I was nineteen or twenty.

"I want you to fuck me," Hannah said, "but I'm looking for more than just fucking. I'm not looking for a husband. I'll do that in my thirties, maybe my forties. I'm looking for companionship, closeness, a little love. Devotion, all that."

"Sounds nice," I said.

"Yes. It sounds—it sounds nice." She took her panties off. "I'd like you to fuck me," she said. "I want you to."

"Lubricant?" I asked, thinking the last time I'd done this, I had to use a lot of petroleum jelly.

"Spit is fine," Hannah said. She spit into her hand, put her hand between her asscheeks. She spit into her hand again and rubbed the saliva over my cock. "I'm getting impatient," she said.

I moved on top of her, feeling inexpert. Hannah reached back, took my cock, and guided me into her ass—where it slid in just fine, without hesitation or resistance. The warmth of her interior sent a tingle up my body and soul. Hannah whispered, "Oh, boy," and pushed her rear up, hard, slamming into my pelvis. I looked down at the streak in her hair, which was scattered about the back of her neck and on the bed with the rest of her hair. I can't swear she had an orgasm, I wasn't sure, but mine came quickly, and it was a lot; I emptied myself inside her.

We lay next to each other after, and Hannah commented on the amount of semen I'd gushed out, that she liked how it felt up her ass and coming out her ass.

She touched and played with my cock and balls, and soon I was hard again. She got on top of me. "This position is always tricky," she said, sitting down on my cock and sliding it in. She leaned forward to kiss me, and it popped out, covered in semen from that first ejaculation. Hannah giggled and put my cock back in her. I reached for the light. "What are you doing?" she said.

"I want to see you."

"I like the light off."

"Okay."

"Oh, turn it on if you want."

I did. She still wore her bra; her hair was a mess. I reached to unclasp her bra and she pushed my hand away; my cock slipped out of her.

"Let's try it like this," I said, gently pushing her off me and onto her back. I put her legs on my shoulders; I didn't need her help to find my way in. I was deep in her now.

"I like this," she said.

"I can kiss you," I said, and did.

"Kiss me more."

I did.

"Fuck me harder."

I did, and I came inside her again.

"I have to piss," I said to her. "Do you want it?"

She made a noise, reached up and bit my right nipple, hard.

"Ouch," I said.

We went back to bed, in each other's arms, and fell asleep.

I woke up, the next morning, with Hannah messing around with my ass. She had her face down there—I was lying sideways—licking from my balls to my crack. I'm not sure how long she'd been doing this, but it was a nice thing to wake up to. She pushed me onto my stomach, spreading my buttocks, a light finger on my sphincter, then a tongue. She licked it a bit, asked me if I liked that. I did, of course— "Yes," I said. She said, "I like it, too," and licked more, harder this time, pushing the tip of her tongue into me like a thirsty animal at a waterhole. I felt saliva roll down onto my balls—a funny, ticklish feeling. She started to suck, making sounds that I can only describe as pleasantly perverse. She did this for the good part of an hour, as I lay there in ecstasy, having discovered a new world. She was still making wicked sucking sounds, and there was a soft hum from the back of her throat.

"My mouth is getting tired," she said. "Can you fuck me?"

She got on her hands and knees, and I took her from behind. I grabbed her hips and slammed myself inside and out of her. I wanted to come in her mouth, this image was in my head, but I couldn't hold out.

And that's how I ended my period of celibacy.

ALISON TYLER

ASHES AND DIAMONDS

H E'S NOT LOOKING AT ME. He's not looking at anything.

"You know what to do. What I *want* you to do."

It's just me and him in the room. I understand fully what it feels like to be taken like this. And I know what it feels like to *want* to be taken like this. To want and to be denied. So I start to slide that slippery toy between the fine cheeks of his ass, and I feel hot tears streaking my cheeks for no reason at all. And Jack says, "Jesus fucking Christ, kid. What do you think I want from you? You think *this* is what I want?"

I'm helpless. The tears are blinding me. But my craving to please overpowers the fear. I don't want to fail. Jack's boyfriend wouldn't fail. But Alex is physically attached to his cock, while mine is synthetic and blue. Silly color choice, that. What the fuck was I thinking? That he wanted something cute? That he craved something artsy?

Jack is waiting.

And I'm letting him down.

His voice is sandpaper rough when he speaks again. He sounds distant, and yet I know the power contained in the man right in front of me. "Don't make me ask again." A simple statement. One that's impossible to ignore.

I swallow hard. It takes everything left in me to grip on to him, to thrust forward, to let him feel it—that's all he wants. I understand. To feel what I feel. He wants to climb inside me, and there's no way for him to actually do that. He wants to climb inside my body, to own every single part of me. To see what makes my mind work. To feel the rush of the blood in my head.

And the blood *is* rushing.

I can't hear anything else but the sound of my own heartbeat. But I'm fucking him, finally. And maybe I understand a little bit about Jack when I do this. Maybe I climb into *his* skin for a moment, seeing my man submitting to me. Even if it's all a big act. Even if Jack could switch the power in a heartbeat, pull forward, take control. But he doesn't. It is a total display of trust that he lets me continue, and I start to feel the pulse beating only in my cunt. Start to feel the wetness and the heat take over. My fingernails grip Jack's skin, and then I press my body to his, my front to his back, and even while my hips are still bucking, I reach under him and touch his cock.

Just a light touch at first.

He groans, his head down, and that sound takes me to a higher level. I grip on to his cock, start to jerk him, touching him like he needs.

He says, "Jesus—" again, but it's different this time. He says, "Jesus," and I know that means "Don't stop."

I'm fucking him hard, and he just takes it all. The pleasure from my fist and the sensation of being filled and the whole fucked-up scene. He devours it, somehow, from beneath. Until *I'm* the one to let go. I'm the one to come, that toy cock pressed so hard against my clit as I fuck him, the feeling of his rocklike rod in my fist. I come until I can hardly breathe, collapsed against him, liquid, spent.

Jack's in motion before I can think. He pulls forward, flips me around, undoes the harness like a pro, and in seconds I'm on my stomach on the mattress. He doesn't use lube. He just fucks. Hard and fast. As if erasing the previous minutes. As if demolishing everything we've done tonight.

He fucks me like a machine, and when he comes, the room seems filled with the light you sometimes see through cut-glass windows. Shivers of light. Diamonds of light.

Or maybe that's just the look of the world through my tears.

ABOUT THE EDITOR

ALLED "A TROLLOP WITH A LAPTOP" by *East Bay Express*, Alison Tyler is naughty and she knows it. Ms. Tyler is the author of more than twenty explicit novels, including *Learning to Love It*, *Strictly Confidential*, *Sweet Thing*, *Sticky Fingers*, and *Something About Workmen* (all published by Black Lace), as well as *Rumors*, *Tiffany Twisted* and *With or Without You* (Cheek). Her novels and short stories have been translated into Japanese, Dutch, German, Italian, Norwegian and Spanish.

Ms. Tyler's short stories in multiple genres have appeared in many anthologies as well as in *Playgirl* magazine and *Penthouse Variations*.

She is the editor of *Batteries Not Included* (Diva); *Heat Wave, Best Bondage Erotica* volumes 1 & 2, *The Merry XXXmas Book of Erotica*, *Luscious*, *Red Hot Erotica*, *Slave to Love*, *Three-Way*, *Happy Birthday Erotica*, *Caught Looking* (with Rachel Kramer Bussel), and *Got a Minute?*

(all from Cleis Press); *Naughty Fairy Tales from A to Z* (Plume); and the *Naughty Stories from A to Z* series, the *Down & Dirty* series, *Naked Erotica* and *Juicy Erotica* (all from Pretty Things Press). Please visit www.prettythingspress.com or www.alisontyler.blogspot.com.